Covert Santa

Danette Fogarty

Dear Readers:

The Christmas books are always a special treat for me to write. I am a huge fan of the holiday season and wish the best for all of you and your families during this Blessed time. Thank you for sharing Karissa and Lane's story and may all your holiday wishes come true.

Love,

Danette

This book is dedicated to the men and women who are away from home for the holidays, protecting us, and their families who miss them.

Also, to my high school English/Drama teacher, Marlene Gottfried. You were a great inspiration!
Thank you!

May the joy of the holiday season fill your heart and bring you peace!

Chapter 1

"Come on, Karissa, please?" Terri asked yet again. She refused to give up until her friend gave in to her request, even if it mean begging.

Sighing, Karissa closed her eyes and tried to keep the headache, that threatened to engulf her entire head, off. "Fine," She finally said, giving in. "I'll write your brother. But," She wanted everything to be above board, "I want it duly noted that I don't think your brother will find any letter from me to be very interesting and I'm sure he's got more important things to do."

Smiling, and jumping up and down as quietly as she could in her classroom, Terri replied, "I will note your reservations." Her students were trickling back into the classroom from lunch, so Terri had to end her call. "I'll email you his address, gotta go, bye," she said and hung up.

Karissa sat at her desk for a few more minutes and wondered what she'd just agreed to.

By the end of the day, Karissa had, as promised, received Terri's brother's mailing address. She dutifully put in in her phone and physical address book.

Organization was a very important part of her job and Karissa put it to use in all areas of her life. He co-workers thought she was a little excessive, but the authors she worked with seemed to appreciate her attention to detail.

As a children's book editor, it

fell to Karissa to pick the books that would appeal to readers and help the authors mold them into sellable pieces of work. So far, she'd been one of the top editors in the firm she worked for. Her intention was to keep that up. In being so committed to her work though, she found her social life slipping into sad shape. Maybe that's why she'd agreed to the crazy idea of Terri's. Writing to man she didn't even know......the whole thing was very un-Karissa-like.

Putting the letter-writing out of her mind, she packed up her bag to leave work.

The drive home was torment, not surprising considering she needed to navigate the traffic in Houston, TX at rush hour.

When she arrived home, she

tossed her bag onto a small bench near the front door.

"Honey, I'm home," She yelled out to no one, and sighed when the silence met her in return.

Going into her bedroom, Karissa stripped off her work clothes and put on her pajama pants and an oversized t-shirt. In an effort to not feel like a total loser, she ate a salad for dinner, but followed it up with a small bowl of ice cream as she caught up on the shows she'd taped from the previous week.

That was her Friday night indulgence, catching up on shows she was too busy to watch Monday through Thursdays.

Sitting on her sofa, she looked around her lovely apartment in an upscale area of Houston. She affectionately called it her tidy little hideaway. The urge to cry snuck up on her and was something new. Maybe writing to Terri's brother was what she needed to get out of the emotional rut that threatened to consume her these days. She was only twenty-seven for crying out loud! Her life shouldn't be so lonely.

Taking a deep breath, she paused her show and got up to find her stationary.

A few minutes later, sitting at her tidy desk, pen in hand, Karissa wondered what she should write. "Just do this," she said aloud to herself and started writing. After a few sentences, she decided it would be faster, and easier if she typed the letter. She got out her laptop and typed it up quickly......

June 12, 2015
Dear Staff Sgt. Huff:

My name is Karissa Godfried, and I'm a friend of your sister, Terri. She guilt-tripped me into writing you, well, sort of. She assures me that you are a great letter writer but never come home so I'll never have to meet you in person. Basically, she's setting us up in her own convoluted way. wro

As far as me, since I'm sure you're just dying to know......NOT, I'm a children's book editor. Thrilling work, as I'm sure you can imagine. I met Terri at a seminar for children's literature. Those 3rd grade teachers sure know what will hook the kids.

Anyway, Terri tells me that you are in the middle of a nine month deployment to Afghanistan. To be honest with you, I'm not sure why

we're still over there. It's not that I'm
anti-American, because I'm proud of
those, like yourself, who choose to put
their lives on the line. It's just that it
seems so distant and far-removed from
everything here.

She says what you do is Top
Secret so she's not even sure what it is.
I find that so fascinating since I can't
seem to keep a secret to save my soul,
other than the books I'm working on.
But, with it being so critical there, it's
probably not a big stretch to just keep it
hush hush.

It's June here and getting hot
already. Since I'm not familiar with
Afghanistan's climate, I'm hoping you'll
give me a synopsis (sorry, editor speak)
of it.

I'm a decent looking woman, I

guess. I'm not like Heidi Klum or anything but I've never had a guy say he was repulsed by me, so I take that as a good sign. I'd include a picture but that's far too personal for a first date, er, letter. Terri described you as big, broad, and with dark hair. She actually used the words Teddy Bear. I felt that was pretty cool since I had a teddy bear that I dearly loved during my childhood. His name was Fred and he was the softest and most cuddliest bear in the world. My brother, Mark, tore him to bits by feeing him to the neighbor's dog when I was ten and I've never gotten over it.

Well, I'm not sure what else to say, except, I'll pray for you every night before I go to sleep. I pray that you and every other service man and woman come home to their loved ones safely. In reality, I understand that this won't happen, but I sure do hope.

Please be safe. I'd like to think of you sitting in front of a computer and typing or something equally safe, all day.

You are more than welcome to write me back, although I'm not really expecting it. It was nice to "meet" you.

Best Wishes,
Karissa

After re-reading the letter several times, checking for both grammatical and spelling errors, Karissa decided this was as good as it was going to get. She printed out the letter.

Before she could change her

mind, she sealed the letter, put the stamp on it, and ran down to the outgoing mail slot on the first floor of her building.

For the rest of the evening, Karissa watched her television shows and thought about what Staff Sgt. Lane Huff would think of her letter.

"Staff Sergeant!" Someone yelled, and Lane turned around. He'd been cranky all morning, probably from lack of sleep and crappy food, but he'd survive.

He was at a decent base, with good security, internet, and showers. It was more than others had so Lane counted himself as lucky. He waited for the Corporal who called him to catch up, and asked, "What's up?"

The Corporal handed him a letter and said, "Nice handwriting," before turning around and walking away.

Lane shook his head. The guys here found all sorts of things here to amuse themselves, including trying to figure out if mail was from a family member or girlfriend so they could tease accordingly.

Looking down at the letter he held, Lane frowned. He didn't recognize the name or address on the envelope. He opened it quickly, reading as he walked.

He'd just finished reading the last sentence when he was at the door to his quarters. It wasn't the

Ritz, but it was sturdy and afforded privacy.

Smiling for the first time today, Lane knew it was because of the letter he got from Karissa Godfried.

Luckily, the other guys who shared his bunkhouse, were out. He got to his makeshift room and closed the door before sitting down at his computer.

Since she typed her letter, he'd do the same.

After re-reading her letter again, he tried to figure out what Karissa Godfried was about. It took a few minutes for him to compose his thoughts, but then he started typing......

June 24, 2015
Dear Karissa,

Imagine my surprise in receiving such a.......well, honest and revealing letter from a woman I've never met. Terri didn't say a word about you in her letters and emails, so I don't even know the basics.

You are right, I can't tell you exactly what I do so let's pretend it's what you imagined; me sitting at a computer and typing up documents. Maybe we'll both rest a little easier with that on our minds.

I have been complimented on my letter-writing abilities, sure, but that's to my family and close friends. Since you're practically a stranger, and book editor no less, I'm feeling a little pressure to find just the right words.

Teddy bear, eh? I've never been

called that to my face before, so I'll have to talk to Terri about that. I'd rather she used a more masculine description such as panther, tiger, lion, possibly even grizzly bear, but that's an "on the ledge" kind of thing.

So, let's make a pact now, no pictures and nothing too personal just yet. Of course, by that, I mean, let's keep writing. I enjoyed your letter. Sarcasm must be one of your more valued traits, or did I interpret the letter wrong? Just checking. I've been known to use it myself and am pretty good about recognizing it, even in a letter.

I hope to hear from you soon.

Best Wishes,
Staff Sgt. Lane Huff

As soon as Lane finished the

letter and put it into an envelope, he heard a few of his guys come into the building. Within a minute, one of his friends, Staff Sgt. Kenston, poked his head into Lane's doorway and asked, "What's up?"

"Just finishing writing a letter," Lane answered, and put the letter into his pocket. No need for his fellow Marines to tease him yet about a woman he got a letter from.

After nodding to Lane, Kenston replied, "Cool, say hi to your sister from me," and left.

Lane rolled his eyes. Kenston had a crush on his sister, Terri, and kept asking Lane to give him Terri's address. Knowing what they did, and that there were no guarantees of safety, Lane hadn't done it yet. This was his second tour over here and he'd lost guys on the first tour. He didn't want Terri to feel that kind of pain, so he shied away from giving her address to anyone serving.

Shrugging, Lane put on his cover and left his room to walk over to the makeshift base post office.

Chapter 2

Karissa was getting home from a particularly grueling day when she walked up to her mailbox. Normally it was filled with advertisements since she paid her bills online. She hated wasting paper and wasn't sure if that was linked to her OCD or being an editor. Either way, she was shocked when, in the box, there was a letter from the Staff Sgt.

Something happened inside; excitement flooded her chest, and she grabbed the mail before practically running up to her apartment.

Once inside, she didn't even kick off her shoes before tearing open the envelope.

Smiling, she noticed that he'd typed his letter too.

After reading it once, Karissa

put it down long enough to change out of her work clothes and into her yoga clothes.

Even after receiving the letter, it was still Tuesday, and that meant yoga for an hour.

When the hour was up, Karissa gladly quit. Normally doing the yoga poses centered her, but not today. Today she wanted to re-read the Staff Sgt.'s letter and then write him back.

Not bothering to shower and change, she walked to her desk and began the letter to him......

July 7, 2015
Dear Staff Sgt. Huff:

I'm sorry your sister didn't tell you about me. Actually, that perturbs me. Geez, she sets us up and doesn't even sing my praises to you? Some friend she is.

It was a lovely surprise to get your letter. Doubly so because this week has already been full of stress. I'm working with a new author on her first book and let's just say, it's tense. The book concept is great, and her writing is wonderful, but her personality is a little too eccentric for my taste. Anyway, getting your letter and reading it, and especially seeing the part where you hope to hear from me again, really made my day.

Since we're no longer strangers technically, I will disclose that I am a creature of habit (as if you didn't suspect as much already). I plan, and plan, and plan some more. I would love to tell you that I'm spontaneous and adventurous, but that would be a lie.

My idea of living it up is skipping

my workout or taking a different route to work. Boring, right?

I guess I shouldn't explain my shortcomings right away and chase you off. Sorry about that. Let's start again.. I skydive, bungee jump, and climb mountains. Ah……no! I have done some travelling but that was for work so does it really count?

I did note that you forgot to give me the climate information I asked for in my letter, so I'll ask again.

Things here are warm and warming up by the day. Ahhhhh, the south. I wasn't born here, I was born in California and moved down here after college to take a job with the firm I currently work for.

It took a while for me to acclimate myself to Texas, but I do like it. The people here are friendly and I've made some friends, like Terri, who are very cool.

I'm having lunch with her next week and she'd going to hear about her lack of promoting my many virtues to you.

By the way, Happy Fourth of July! Sorry it's late. I did watch fireworks on tv and wondered if you were able to do the same, probably not though.

Please stay safe and know I'm thinking of you.
Karissa

Just like she did after writing the first letter, Karissa sealed up the envelope and ran it downstairs to the outgoing mailbox. It was important to get it out and she wasn't sure why since the mailperson didn't come until late morning and it was a little after seven in the evening.

Once the letter was mailed though, Karissa felt like she was able to calm down enough and actually did some more yoga.

At bedtime she was able to settle down quickly with a smile on her face.

For some reason, she dreamed of teddy bears.

Returning back from a security detail, Lane was dusty and parched. He went straight to the mess tent to get some water. After grabbing a bottle, he spotted Kenston and a few of his other buddies so he walked over to them and sat down.

"Any issues?" Kenston asked his friend.

Lane shook his head no and answered, "Nothing too bad."

Bad could be measured on a lot of different levels. This time around, he was at a different base and there were different missions to complete. Never once did he, or the Marines he worked with, take for granted that things were safe, so they were always keyed up when they left for a mission. Lane was just glad that he was back and in one piece.

Kenston nodded in understanding and then told his friend, "Hey, I got your mail for you," he handed a letter to Lane and laughed while saying, "writing your sister my butt."

Giving Kenston a glare, Lane took the letter and put it in his pocket before getting up and walking over to get some lunch.

He stayed at the mess tent with his buddies for another twenty minutes, but his mind was on the letter practically burning a hole in his pocket. When he sent the reply to Karissa's first letter, he wasn't sure that she would write back. He'd read the letter so many times that the paper was worn.

Finally finishing his lunch, Lane made his way back to his room. He tore open the letter as soon as his door was closed and started to read it.

Smiling at her sarcasm and witty wording, Lane was excited to write her back. He got out his laptop and started typing right away..........

July 12, 2015
Dear Karissa,

Okay, first things first, it's about 95 degrees here during the day and a lot colder at night. It's kind of dry now, with the winter being over. Nothing spectacular about the weather here and definitely not as wet or humid as Houston.

As far as Terri's lack of promoting you to me, well, the woman works with kids aged 7-9 years old. I imagine her brain is almost fried. Plus, she's dating that professor and I'm not sure about him yet. And, as if all of that wasn't enough, you did a great job of telling me about yourself so don't worry about what Terri has to say.

I have to divulge that my buddies saw your letter and know that I'm writing to someone back home now. I'm getting some flak for it, but it doesn't bother me much. Your letters make me smile. Please don't stop writing.

There is something soothing about knowing that someone is thinking about you, don't you agree? At the oddest moments, I'll think of you and wonder if you're thinking of me. Is that too personal? I don't want to scare you off with my words. I just know that I don't wait to say what I think anymore. I used to, you know, I thought I had all the time in the world but not anymore. Not after being here. Just know that I'm here thinking about you. By the way, how many letters do we have to exchange before I get a picture? Let me know.

Take care of yourself.
Lane

Karissa got ready for work, her lunch date weighing heavily on her mind. She wanted to ask her friend a million questions about her brother, but then again, she wanted to figure out some things for herself. It was weird, this feeling of knowing someone when you only exchanged a few letters.

The morning was filled with meetings and Karissa was relieved when it was over.

She had two new writers that she was working with, in addition to her other established writers. It was a juggling act to be sure.

When Karissa arrived at the restaurant, she spotted Terri right away. Her friend always wore a smiled and Karissa wished she was as carefree as Terry seemed to be. "Hello, there," She greeted Terri as she walked up to the table.

Terri stood and hugged Karissa tightly. They were both busy and tried so hard to fit in visits. Sometimes it was months between them. They hadn't seen one another since March, and it was already July.

As they both sat down, Terri asked, "Okay, how is writing to Lane going?"

Deciding to tease her friend just a bit, Karissa came back with, "Who? Your brother? Oh, I completely forgot, I'm sorry. Been busy, you know." She rushed the words for effect and the look on Terri's face was priceless. Not able to keep up the façade, Karissa laughed and said, "Just kidding." She gave Terri a side glance, adding, "But I'm mad at you that you didn't tell him I was writing."

"Honestly," Terri looked a little ashamed, "I wasn't sure you would, so I didn't want to get his hopes up."

Nodding, Karissa couldn't blame her friend for that. It wasn't something she would normally do. In answering Terri's original question about writing Lane, she said, "It's been fun writing him. He seems really likeable, but it's difficult to tell from letters."

Picking up on Karissa's plural use, Terri beamed, before saying, "So you've been sending them?" She asked.

With a sigh, Karissa gave her friend a dry look, but responded, "Yes, if you must know, we've exchanged a few. I just hate waiting for them to reach him, him reply, and then getting them back to me."

Leaning back in her chair, her arms crossed across her chest, Terri looked smug. "You know," She said slowly, "there's this lovely little invention called email," she tried to look encouraging, "and it gets letters back and forth a heck of a lot faster."

Feeling a little foolish, Karissa shot back, "Well, I didn't know he had access to it, and he didn't mention it."

They ordered their lunch and then Terri pulled out a notepad and wrote down Lane's email address for Karissa.

The rest of the lunch was fun,

catching up on Terri's plans for the upcoming school year and hearing about the kids she tutored over the summer. They did discuss a few of Karissa's projects but only on a general level since she couldn't divulge specifics on unreleased works.

"So," Terri commented when their plates were being removed, "you seem a little happier when you talk about Lane."

Blushing, Karissa looked down and refolded the cloth napkin on her lap. She wasn't sure how to respond. "I am," She admitted, "his letter was a little vague, but it came on a day when I really needed a break from my life."

Understanding the sentiment,

Terri offered, "Amen to that."

They finished up their lunch and parted ways outside of the restaurant. Terri promised to email Lane and let him know she gave his email address to Karissa.

Chapter 3

Lane did his daily duties and then decided to check his email before he hit the rack for sleep. The day was a long one and he was tired. He opened up his laptop, logged in, and pulled up his email. First up was an email from Terri so he read it......

To: LHuff1988@email.com
From: Number1teacher12@email.com
Subject: I'm sorry

Lane:

I just had lunch with Karissa a few hours ago and I'm sorry I didn't tell you about her writing to you. As I explained to her, I wasn't sure she would really go through with it, so I didn't want to get your hopes up. Please forgive me.

I haven't told mom about your letter writing so I should get points for that, right?

Anyway, I gave Karissa your email address today to make it easier for you two to communicate. You're welcome, by the way. I love you big brother and you be safe or I'll come over there and kick your butt.

P.S. Karissa's email is KGodfried@HCB.com, it's her work email so she checks it like 100 times a day.

Love,
Terri

Lane smiled as he finished reading his sister's email. She was right and he would thank her……. Eventually. He didn't know why he didn't offer the email option to Karissa right away. It seemed a little more mysterious getting physical letters. But Terri was right, this was faster.

He pulled out the last letter he'd gotten from Karissa and reread it. He wanted to wait until he got an email from her first. She should have gotten his last letter or would be getting it soon. Maybe this would be a way to share a little more about one another.

As he turned off his bedside light, Lane felt nervous excitement, and smiled until he fell asleep.

The day that Karissa saw Lane's letter in her mailbox, she practically jumped for joy. She'd had his email for almost a week but was still too chicken to send him one. Not sure why, she just knew she was.

When she got up to her apartment, she dropped her bag and purse by the door, sat down at the small kitchen table, and opened up the letter.

His words were wonderful and made Karissa feel very warm inside. Absently, she raised her hand to her cheek, and knew from its warmth that she was blushing.

All day long, she worked with words, and yet, Lane's words made her feel more than any of the ones she read at work. He was thinking about her....that thought blew her mind.

She imagined that he was a teddy bear, at least on the inside.

After making herself put he letter down, she got her phone out of her purse and pulled up his email address to write him back.

Sitting down in her little office, she pulled out her laptop and began writing……..

To: LHuff1988@email.com
From: KGodfried@HCB.com
Subject: This is faster, I hope it's okay.

Dear Lane,

I hope that it's okay that I dropped the formality of Staff Sgt. and just used your first name. I noticed you use my name in on your letters and it makes it more personal.

I received your letter today and practically ran upstairs to my apartment to read it. You most certainly DO NOT scare me off with your words. Actually, they make me feel special. That's not a normal thing for me, really. As I explained, I'm pretty boring so it's not like I've got men banging at the door and asking me out.

Having someone thinking about you is pretty awesome so thank you for thinking about me. As far as pictures go, I'm not sure I'm quite ready to take that leap yet so I hope you understand.

Terri felt somewhat bad but explained that she was afraid I'd chicken out on writing you. Also, not too far off of the mark. Isn't it strange that I did write? I think so.

Thank you for the climate information on Afghanistan. I know I could've just googled it but hearing about it from you makes it a little more real.

How would you like to do this? Do you want to only email once a week or more often? I don't want to interrupt your schedule, but I do have questions for you.

Please know that you're in my thoughts and prayers every day.
Be safe!

Karissa

Lane woke up at five in the morning. It was his usual routine so, even on his days off duty, he still woke up at the same time. His birthday was in a few weeks, and he expected an onslaught of letters and emails from his mother and sister asking what he wanted them to send him. Personally, he thought of his birthday as just another day, but they made a big deal out of it every year and there was no way to stop that.

Getting out of bed, he rubbed his sleepy eyes and sat down at his desk to boot up his laptop.

When he looked at his inbox, Lane smiled. There was an email from Karissa. He greedily read her words, then read the email a second time to absorb everything she said.

Her words spoke of someone who was shy and tentative about personal things. He could relate to that on a lot of levels. Her honesty made his chest tighten in a strange way that he couldn't describe. Shutting down his laptop, Lane wanted to think about a reply before he wrote back.

The mess hall was packed by the time he got there, so he tried to get his food and eat quickly so he could get back to his room and reply to Karissa's email.

His friend Kenston sat down as he was finishing up his meal, and asked, "What's up?"

Shrugging, Lane tried to be standoffish in the hopes his friend would get the subtle message to leave him alone. Unfortunately,

Kenston wasn't really into subtlety.

"So, how's the woman you're writing?" Kenston asked Lane.

Nodding in a non-committal way, Lane gave his friend a small smile, and answered, "She's good." All of a sudden, it occurred to Lane that he could take care of two things at once, so he suggested to Kenstion, "Why don't you write to my sister?"

Surprised, Kenston sat there, looking startled for almost a minute. He finally muttered, "Wh, wh, what?"

Smiling, Lane clapped his friend on the shoulder, and explained, "You keep giving me crap about writing to someone, so now you can do it too, and leave me

 be." He failed to mention that this was also a little payback for Terri's pushing Karissa into writing him. Not that he regretted that, but still, his
sister needed a little taste of her own medicine. Plus, she'd told him a few days earlier that she wasn't seeing that professor guy anymore.

Taking out a small pad of paper and pen he kept on him, Lane wrote down Terri's email address and slid the paper across the table to Kenston. "Write her," he said and got up to leave the mess tent.

When he got back to his room, Lane felt a little bad, but only a very little bit, about giving Kenston Terri's email. He sat down and started writing his own reply to Karissa…….

To: KGodfried@HCB.com

From: LHuff1988@email.com
Subject: No problem

Dear Karissa,

It was a fluke that I checked my email this morning and I'm so glad I did.

First of all, write as often as you want to. I really like us writing back and for the and email really does make it so much faster. You're right, I feel silly for not thinking of it sooner.

The excitement you describe when you receive my letters is something I really get. I feel it too. Getting the letter is cool, but this way, I can just shoot you a quick one if I'm short on time or think of a question I think is important.

Terri is Terri and I'm pretty sure she won't change.

I have an admission to make. In an effort to get my friend off my back and give my sister a taste of her own medicine, I gave my friend, Kenston, her email address and told him to write her. Am I awful?

Today I'm off duty so I get to veg. The internet connection is pretty reliable here so I'm able to catch up on tv shows that aired in the U.S. or play video games (a popular way to pass the time over here) or email.

I know what you mean about thinking about someone. My big question is.......how can you feel so excited about someone you've never seen or met? Not that I'm pressuring you, I'm just a little shaken at how quickly I look forward to our letters.

Please write soon. I'd like to know more about your job. Is it stressful? I know you mentioned an author, how does that work? I am truly interested.

I hope to hear from you soon. Waiting impatiently,

Lane

As he pushed the "send" button at the bottom of the email, Lane wished he'd said something more interesting. After re-reading the email, he sounded a little lame. Who would've thought it?

Laying down on his rack, Lane stared at the ceiling of his small room and wondered what Karissa looked like.

Karissa was getting ready for bed. She googled the time difference between Houston and Afghanistan and discovered there was a ten- and one-half hour time difference. When she emailed him earlier, it was far to early for him to be up and writing back.

Trying to focus on her nightly

routine, she was distracted with thoughts of Lane and what he was doing. Before going to bed, she decided to check her email once more, and was shocked to see a reply from Lane. It was only seven in the morning there at the time he sent the email.

Reading his words, Karissa tried to get a mental picture of him. It as difficult since she knew nothing of what his job entailed. She would make sure to ask more in the next email.

Chapter 4

It was early August and the Houston heat threatened to engulf the city, and Karissa along with it.

She tried to get to work earlier during the summer so she could get through the early morning reprieve of the hundred plus degrees.

From Lane's emails, he was experiencing the same temperatures, but with the desert there, he didn't feel the sting of the oppressive humidity.

As soon as she reached her desk, Karissa pulled up her email. Sure enough, there was an email from Lane. It was a ritual she started without realizing it.

Just saying his name in her head made her smile. And she didn't care who knew it. She hadn't announced her "pen pal" relationship to anyone but it was becoming apparent that something was going on.

The last time she called her parents, her mother asked her point-blank if she was seeing someone. When Karissa told her, "No," her mother became so quiet. Karissa thought she was probably in shock.

She wasn't telling lies since she never actually met Lane so there was no way she could "see" him. That was her rationalization for the moment, and she was sticking with it.

Lately, she'd been trying to get the nerve up to ask more personal questions of Lane. She'd been wondering a few things for a while, but so far, had yet to ask. Questions would pop into her head at the oddest moments, too. Just the other day, she was in a meeting with an author and wondered if she was the only woman that Lane was writing too. It just came to her out of the blue and she had to really focus to get back on track with the meeting.

Pushing her current insecurities aside, Karissa read his email.........

To: KGodfried@HCB.com
From: LHuff1988@email.com
Subject: Pictures?

Dear Karissa,

It's occurred to me that we've yet to exchange pictures. I know you've thought about it too, but I wanted to know what your opinion is about it now that we've been writing back and forth for months.

If you don't want to, I would understand. I would also be lying if I didn't say that my curiosity isn't piqued, (did you like my use of that word, editor lady?). I imagine what you look like, given your rather vague description in your first letter but it leaves a lot of gaps. If you haven't noticed, the different between Heidi Klum, and let's say, the hunchback of Notre Dame is pretty vast.

Besides, in my defense, I don't want to be known as a teddy bear. I could bean Terri for even using that particular description. I consider myself a warrior.

Now that I've given you my reasoning behind the request of a picture, let's move on.

Today was another blissful day (sarcasm) in this spa-like setting. I got another paper cut from typing my fingers to the bone.

Actually, we did well today, accomplished what we needed to do, and everyone is safe. As soon as I get back to my room, I check my email to see if there's one from you. It makes me smile to see them.

I'm sorry you're not getting any further in your attempts to be nice to your "eccentric" author. He/she (you haven't specified) sounds like a real doozy. I'll think good thoughts and hope for your continued patience. What is the name of the book he/she is writing anyway? I thought maybe you could at least give me that.

To say I miss you sounds so strange, but it's true. I don't consider myself a man who puts his feelings out there much. No room for that here in my current assignment and normally it isn't a problem. Bur for some reason, I think of you, and it all leaves my head.

Am I too corny? Let me know because although we've been writing for a while, there are still a lot of gaps.

Have you ever broken a bone? Did you wear braces? You've

mentioned your family here and there, but are you close with them?

I guess this email is getting too long and you'll think I am actually a teddy bear if I don't sign off.

Hope to hear from you soon.
Lane

Karissa sat back in her chair and laughed. He was asking questions along the lines of the ones she was thinking of asking him.

Looking out her office door, to make sure Sheila wasn't in yet, Karissa hit the reply button on the email and began typing......

To: LHuff1988@email.com
From: KGodfried@HCB.com
Subject: Interesting

Dear Lane:

I had to chuckle when you were asking questions because I've been meaning to aske some of my own.

First of all, I'll answer yours. I did break my elbow during an unfortunate encounter with a tree when I was twelve. I've broken numerous toes over the years in my laziness to turn on lights when it was dark. That furniture just jumps out at you, doesn't it?

I've never worn braces. Like any normal person, I've got a few teeth that aren't perfectly straight, but I don't look like a piranha or anything like that.

I'm somewhat close to my parents but my siblings are scattered and not as close as we probably should be. From what I get in talking to Terri (and our letters), is that it seems like you and Terri are much closer than I have ever been with my brother and sister. I love them though, and I believe they know that.

As for my questions, they are a bit more personal in nature. If you decide you don't want to answer them, I will understand but I will be disappointed. Up to now, we've kept our letter light. So here goes.....

Am I the only woman you're writing to? Have you had your heart broken? Have you ever been in love?

Like I said, my questions are more intimate and, again, I would understand your reluctance to answer. They (the questions) tend to sneak up on me and I've caught myself, more than once, zoning out and thinking about them, and you.

In regards to my, less than wonderful, author/client, well SHE is in a league of her own. The book she wrote is titled "The Quail With No Tail," and it's adorable. It's about being different and how that's okay, which is a great life lesson. I wish she was able to compromise as well as the characters in her book do. I'm still trudging forward and believe in the book. I will keep you posted.

I like corny! There, I said it. So don't worry about it anymore. When we write, it's as if it's just the two of us. Our lives are here and there and I know it, but when we write, we're in this little bubble that is only the two of us. That's very precious to me.

Another thing, as I said previously, I really loved my teddy bear and if that's the description Terri used, for Heaven's sake man, embrace it! Teddy Bears are strong! They keep you safe when you're afraid of the dark and they hold you tight when you're about to get a shot at the doctor's office. They also soak up your tears when you boyfriend of less than a week dumps you for some other girl in the seventh grade. I think I've made a strong case for the teddy bear.

I haven't forgotten about the picture request, I'm just procrastinating. What if you don't think I look good? And then there's picking out a picture to begin with. Women are weird that way. I think I'll put it to you this way, you show me yours and I'll show you mine. I know that came out sounding perverse, so I'll apologize now.

Please, please, please, be safe. I worry, but I know that as long as I get an email, everything is okay.

Karissa

Karissa pushed the send button then wondered if she should have signed off with some affectionate word at the end of the email. Just putting her name down seemed a little lame, but she couldn't very well put "Best Wishes," or "love," now, could she? There were some things that Lane would need to bring up first. Affectionate titles or send offs would have to be included in that.

Just after she sent the email to Lane, her assistant, Sheila, came into the office and her workday officially began. It felt good to know that Lane would get her email either before he went to bed or when he woke up. There was a crazy excitement in knowing it would be there for him and Karissa found herself smiling even bigger, and happy that no one knew why.

Lane got back to his room and fell into his bunk. They had to do a security escort into one of the less stable areas. There were still a lot of people here who didn't much care for the American military being in their country. Whatever the reasoning, it meant that missions weren't easy.

Even though he was exhausted, Lane opened his eyes and stared up at the ceiling. He thought about Karissa. Just the thought of her, sitting at what he assumed was a neat desk in that publishing firm, made his mouth form into a smile.

Before he could go to sleep, he had to check his email. With he time difference, she tended to write him in the morning there, so he could read her emails before going to bed here. He slept better on the nights when he got an email, which, thankfully, was pretty often now.

Opening up his laptop, Lane found himself feeling nervous. He'd asked her for a photo in his last email to her and wondered if she was ready for that next step. Their relationship wasn't exactly normal, but it worked. He didn't want to question why, but he definitely wanted them both to keep writing.

Luckily, there was an email from her, and Lane opened it up, smiling. He laughed outright at some of her comments and had to remind himself to keep it down. No need to draw attention to himself or disturb his buddies in their own little cubbies.

After reading Karissa's email, Lane started to worry a bit. He understood her point about the picture. Scanning through the pictures on his laptop, he tried to see if any were good enough to send her.

Most of them were of him and

his fellow Marines trying to look manly. None of those seemed appropriate to send to Karissa.

It took him another thirty minutes to find a picture he thought was good. He cropped out the surrounding area and hoped it was clear enough when she saw it.

Without thinking about it any further, he attached the picture, and put in the subject line, "This is me," and sent it.

Chapter 5

It was late and Karissa's stomach was growling. She was exhausted but couldn't leave work just yet.

Her meeting with her "eccentric" author ran way over time and put her out of sorts. The woman was brilliant, but her crazy attitude toward her work was just soaking up Karissa's patience. She'd even spoken to her boss about the friction but, although empathetic, her boss told her that everything had to stay in place. The buzz about the book was encouraging and they did want to publish it. Karissa just had to find a way to deal.

Rubbing her eyes, Karissa was just about done when she thought about Lane. It was if her mind just shut off from work and switched on to him.

Opening her email, Karissa scanned the inbox until she saw the email from Lane that said, "This is me."

She took a deep breath and opened up the email. She paused another second before clicking on the attachment.

The picture came up and Karissa held her breath for a few more seconds. She was so focused on the picture of Lane that she didn't hear her assistant, Sheila, come into her office and move up behind her.

"Here's the contract for Ms. Leonard," She was saying as she rounded Karissa's desk. Her eyes lifted and settled on the computer screen that her boss was looking at. She stopped for a second, smiled, and said, "So this is what's got you smiling for no reason."

Coming out of her trance, Karissa managed to give her assistant a glare. "I don't know what you're talking about," She responded defensively. Closing her email, she turned around to look at Sheila.

Placing the contract on Karissa's desk, Sheila returned the glare, and commented, "You can sell that somewhere else. He's yummy and I knew something was up because you would've told the talented Ms. Leonard to take a hike if you didn't have him making you so distracted.

A flush made its way up into Karissa's cheeks. "We've only been writing and emailing," She explained. "This is the first picture I've seen of him. He wants one of me, and I don't know what to send." Her voice sounded desperate which was ridiculous.

Smiling at her boss, because Sheila was certainly no stranger to the way men could tangle up women's minds, she said, "It's easy, send him the one you had taken for our website here." She nodded toward the laptop. "It's sexy because you've got that kind of half smile going on. He'll think you're mysterious like the Mona Lisa."

Karissa couldn't help but chuckle at the comparison. If only she was a confident in her looks as Sheila was. The idea was a good one though, because the picture was professional but made her look pretty. "Good idea," She commented to Sheila and pulled up the company website to copy and paste the picture into her email.

After attaching the photo into a new email, she put 'This is me,' in the subject line. For some reason, she couldn't push the send button though. When Sheila leaned over her shoulder and pushed it for her, Karissa felt better and told Sheila, "Thanks."

Shaking her head, Sheila walked toward the office door, "I'm off, and you should be too. Mr. Sexy Guy will email you ASAP, so you want to get home quick." She winked and left the office.

Gathering up her bag, and her pride, Karissa took a deep breath and hoped Lane liked her picture as much as she liked his.

When Karissa arrived home, about an hour later, she quickly went back into her email. She didn't see a response from Lane yet, but she did manage to save his picture to her laptop wallpaper, so she'd see him every time she opened up her laptop. Before she sat down to eat dinner, she texted Terri......

Good evening. You didn't tell me that you brother was so handsome. He sent me a picture and I'm blushing. And before you ask, I DID send him one of me.

An hour later, Karissa was at her desk paying some bills when her phone pinged to signal an incoming text. She smiled when she saw it was from Terri......

You never asked if he was handsome so I wasn't obliged to supply that information. ☺

    Laughing at Terri's sassy reply, Karissa texted back......

I see, so now we're splitting hairs. I'll remember that....

    She sent the text but didn't hear back from Terri. Her friend was probably on a date or something and didn't have time to talk.
    As she was getting ready for bed, Karissa wondered if Lane had received her picture. She was pretty sure it would be impossible to sleep until she knew for sure.

Lane woke up, jumped out of bed, and turned on his laptop. He wanted to find out if Karissa got his picture and what she thought.

Slipping on his slippers, a must to keep the sand off of your feet, even indoors, and walked over to sit down at his makeshift desk.

Still waiting for his laptop to load, he decided to run to the restroom. Some things just couldn't wait. He was back in just a few minutes and eagerly clicked on the icon to open up his email. He saw her response immediately and the subject mimicked his with, 'This is me.'

After he clicked on the attachment, he waited for the picture to fill his screen. It only took a few seconds, but it seemed like forever. When the picture loaded,

Lane's breath hitched in his throat. She was almost exactly how her pictured her, only more beautiful. Thinking about it, Lane realized it didn't matter because in the space of seven weeks, since they started writing, he found himself falling in love with Karissa Godfried, a woman he'd never met in person.

Not realizing that he'd left his door partially open when he came back from the bathroom, Lane sat there and stared at her picture, until he heard a whistle from behind him. Jumping, he saw Kenston standing there. "Don't you knock?" He asked his nosy friend.

Kenston snorted, then said, "Dude, the door was open," he looked back at the computer screen and asked, "Who's the babe?"

For the first time in the three years, he'd known Kenston, Lane actually wanted to punch him in the face. "The babe, as you call her, is Karissa, the woman I've been writing to." He glared at Kenston. "And you know that you might get a better reaction from women if you don't disrespect them by calling them, babe."

To his credit, Kenston looked uncomfortable by Lane's tone and words. Lane could only hope it was due to embarrassment. He asked his friend, "Did you send an email to my sister yet?"

Shaking his head, no, Kenston said, "I haven't gotten up the courage to yet."

Lane stood up and smiled at his friend, "Good, that means you're nervous and she's not just some babe to you."

Kenston rolled his eyes and left Lane's room, closing the door behind him.

Turning back around, Lane looked at Karissa's picture again for a few more minutes before he started his email to her.......

To: KGodfried@HCB.com
From: LHuff1988@email.com
Subject: Wow!!!!!!!

Dear Karissa:
     What the heck were you worried about? You're gorgeous!
I didn't see an email from you after I sent you my picture, so I'm worried you think I look like some sort of psycho or something. Our appearance is slightly

altered here during our rotation here to "blend in" better.

Since I now realize I neglected to answer your question yesterday, I'll answer them now.

You are the ONLY woman I'm writing to that I am not related to. That sounded kind of weird so I hope you know what I meant by that. I don't think I've had my heart broken because I've never been in love before. There have been relationships, but nothing too serious. My job is serious enough, to be honest. I didn't want to choose between my career and a relationship.

Thank you for answering my questions, but now I'd like to turn your questions back at you. Am I the only man you're writing to? Have you had your heart broken?
Have you ever been in love?

Just typing the questions makes me a little anxious. I suppose I'm worried that you have had your heart broken and are leery of any relationships. But, then again, if you haven't, am I just a writing fling? Men have feelings too, you know.

I am trying to do as you demanded and "embrace" my teddy bearism. It is not an easy task as pride keeps me on a tight leash, but I am trying. Is it too soon to hope that I could keep you safe at night from monsters, and hold you tight at the doctor's office, and soak up your tears? If so, then I think I would be much happier in accepting the description.

Thank you for the picture, I'll keep it on my wallpaper so I can see you every time I turn on my laptop. Any more you want to send, please do.

I might as well tell you that my buddy, Kenston, saw your picture and called you a "babe." I almost punched him (no lie).

Our current schedule for today is light so I'm hoping to get some rest and stare at your picture for a while. I'll do as you ask and take care, but only because if I don't, I won't be able to see you.

And yes, the stupid furniture does jump out at night and get in the way.

Thinking of you,
Lane

After sending the email, Lane smiled all the way through breakfast. Even when the CO called an unplanned meeting and gave out new directives for their mission, Lane just nodded and smiled. He couldn't help himself.

Karissa woke up the next

morning, and was relieved it was the weekend. She had a list of errands as long as her arm, but at least she could procrastinate a little and stay in bed. The night before, she'd put her laptop on her nightstand, so she didn't have to get out of bed in order to check her emails.

When she saw the email from Lane in her inbox, she smiled, and opened it.

Laying there in her bed, Karissa felt somewhat exposed. His words were like little bubbles of happiness that were popping all around her. Having the subject line say 'Wow,' certainly didn't hurt. And then as she read what he wrote, about her, about him, and about them, she couldn't help but feel tingly all over. She laughed when she read the comment about the furniture and sighed when she read the 'thinking of you,' at the end.

Was this it? Was this the ever-elusive feeling of falling in love? If so, it was strangely intoxicating.

Karissa reread the email three more times before she got out of bed. And today, she didn't even need coffee to get her up and moving.

Chapter 6

The summer seemed to be passing too quickly and Karissa had to put herself mentally in check to make herself enjoy it.

Work could take up as much time as she allowed it to, and she promised herself she would get out and do things that were fun.

Terri called several times and left messages, so Karissa called her back and they made a dinner date.

It was late August, so the days were long and very hot. No one would know that Karissa lived in Texas given her pale skin. She was in the office all of the time it seemed. Even Sheila had started grumbling about her "letting loose."

The day of Karissa's dinner date with Terri arrived and it was a much-needed distraction.

They met up outside of the restaurant and were laughing and hugging while walking inside.

"How are you?" Terri asked as they were shown to their table.

Shrugging, Karissa answered, "Busy at work."

Terri stared at her friend as they settled into their seats. There was definitely something different about Karissa and she would find out how much her brother had to do with that. "So, how's Lane?" She asked.

"He's good," Karissa answered, and smiled. "They are trying to get through the heat over there and do what they can." When she looked up from her menu, and into Terri's knowing look, she blushed. "You tricked me, didn't you?" she asked Terri.

Nodding, Terri just giggled. "I see something, and it wasn't there before." She tilted her head to get a better look at her friend. Karissa almost glowed. "You look…….. happy."

Leaning forward, Karissa admitted, "I only work and email Lane," she smiled shyly, "and I go to bed with him on my mind and wake up with thoughts of him, and oh my………sorry."

Terri laughed, and shook her head, saying, "No need to be sorry." Reaching across the table, she squeezed Karissa's hand, "If anything," she added, "I'm envious."

Karissa smiled back. She was happy, but there were a lot of questions. Questions about what Lane did, what he wanted to do when he was done with his tour in Afghanistan, and what she would do if he wanted to meet. They didn't discuss anything in the future, only the immediate, and it worked, for now.

Dinner was fun and the two friends laughed a lot.

Karissa told Lane all about it in her email that night. They still continued to email daily, something more than once if she had a light day or he was off duty.

To: LHuff1988@email.com

From: KGodfried@HCB.com
Subject: Your sister

Dear Lane:

After weeks of trying to coordinate our schedules, Terri and I were finally able to meet up for dinner tonight. It was such fun, but you were missed. Funny, right? I was thinking that you should be there as we sat and ate our lovely meal.

Speaking of meals, I don't think I asked you how the food is over there. There are a million questions like that one that run through my mind. I'm nervous about asking since we made a sort of unspoken agreement to not delve too deeply into your job over there. Not that the food is necessarily a part of your job, I'm just not sure.

There are more questions, but I'll save those for another day. This week has been rough and I've been putting in more time at work than I should.

I never realize how beat down I am until I find myself exhausted, have you ever noticed that? And then, I feel a little guilty about commenting on my job when, let's face it, my job is nothing compared to yours.

I'm realizing that this email is sounding sad and I'm so sorry about that. I don't mean it to, and I don't want to drag you into my funk.

I hope your day went well and know I'm thinking of you.
Love,
Karissa

It was about an hour later, when Karissa was in her bathroom, brushing her teeth before bed, when she remembered that she signed off the email with the word love.

Her chest started beating erratically and she jumped into bed, pulling the covers up to her chin. "Oh my Lord," she whispered to herself. It wasn't as if she'd done anything awful, but it was more of a realization that she meant to word love.

Lane woke up and turned on his computer while he was getting ready to start the day.

Unfortunately, things were heating up in their area and it was more than just the simmering temperatures of summer. He wasn't worried exactly, but it meant that the scope of their mission could change again.

When he got back to his room, he saw the email from Karissa and smiled.

Her emails always made his day start off on a good note. As he read this particular email though, he frowned. It wasn't like Karissa to be down, and he was worried that she was doing too much.

Not that he knew the first thing about what a children's book editor did, but he was pretty sure, from her emails, that it was mentally taxing.

Already thinking of his reply email, Lane finished reading her email. It was at the end that he saw the word, 'love,' before her name. He actually sat back in his chair and stared at the computer screen.

Never in a million years did he think that Karissa would be the first one of them to end an email with the endearment.

Perhaps if they were a normal dating couple, he would've told her weeks earlier how he felt. But they weren't normal so he understood that things would work a little differently. And, seeing that one word from Karissa, made all the difference to him.

He started to think of things in a different way, forming a plan in his mind.

Karissa slept poorly. She tossed and turned and hoped that Lane wasn't upset about her using the word 'Love' in the email. It was silly, and logically she knew that.

But, there was no reply email from Lane so that gave her a lot of time to think.

On Monday morning, she walked into her office, early yet again. She turned on her work computer and went to get some coffee from the break room.

By the time Karissa got back to her own office, Sheila was at her own desk, smiling.

"You're here early," Karissa

said to her assistant, hoping her
voice sounded calmer than she
actually felt.

Sheila smiled back, and
answered, "I am here because you
are here, and I know you come in
early every morning so you can read
an email from Mr. Hunky Guy
before you start work. "

Frowning, Karissa felt bad
because Sheila was right, but not
having heard from Lane in two days
was driving her nuts. "How did
you know I did that?" She asked
Sheila as she walked into her own
office, with Sheila hot on her heels.

Standing there, Sheila crossed
her arms and asked, "What's up?
I've worked for you for almost five
years now and you are nothing if

not a creature of habit."

Karissa wouldn't dispute it since it was true. But today, her nerves were really getting to be overwhelming. "Well, I think I screwed up and made a mistake. I signed an email, Love."

Rolling her eyes, but still smiling, Sheila said, "It's about time."

Very confused, Karissa plopped down into her desk chair. "What do you mean," She asked Sheila.

Sheila leaned forward, and replied, "You are a beautiful, talented, and driven woman, Karissa, and you're in love." She smiled and went on, "But you're the last one to see it."

"And here I thought you were going to regale me with pearls of wisdom," Karissa returned, her voice full of sarcasm.

Sheila, shaking her head and sighing, just said, "I just did."

Watching her assistant leave her office, Karissa waited until the door was shut behind Sheila before she let out a breath.

Looking at her computer, she opened up her email and searched for one from Lane. When she saw there was one there, she was almost hyperventilating. Clicking to open up the document, she started reading it.

To: KGodfried@HCB.com

From: LHuff1988@email.com
Subject: You sound sad

Dear Karissa,

When you write sad things, I just want to take you into my arms and hold you tight. I know we said nothing too personal, but I'm throwing that out now. Whatever you want to ask, please ask. I'll do the same.

You sounded exhausted in your email. You need to take care of yourself. No use in running yourself down physically or mentally. Do you want me to send some "friends" to your office to take care of any unruly authors or coworkers you may have? I can do that you know.

I hope that made you smile.

Please tell me about your apartment, I think of this tidy little place with small furnishings and a lot of neutral tones. Am I right?

I'll include a pic of my "sleep cubicle" here so you can see what it's like. As a disclaimer, the pictures on the wall are of Terri, my parents, and some of my buddies. I didn't want you to think I have pictures of women up there.

If I'm honest, I'll admit that my heart skipped a beat when I read the word, 'love,' at the end of your email. It was as if I received the most precious gift. Do you realize that your writing to me is a gift? It is, and every day that I get to read words you've written, I feel like the luckiest man in the world.

Feel better and email me when you can.
Love,
Lane

By the time Karissa finished reading the last paragraph of the email, she was crying. Luckily, her mascara was waterproof. But the same couldn't be said for her heart. It was sensitive and Lane's words definitely made it beat faster.

Chapter 7

A month later, Karisssa was absorbed in reading a press release her office was going to send out regarding her author's new book, "The Quail With No Tail."

The book release was on schedule and the initial reviews from the focus groups were great.

Terri was one of the lucky teachers to get the book in advance and read it to her class the first day of school. She made sure to let Karissa know what the class thought and questions the kids asked after having it read to them.

The author, Ms. Leonard, was getting more tolerable, or maybe it was Karissa who was becoming more tolerable. She used to have to take at least ten minutes after a meeting with Ms. Leonard just to get her nerves settled. Now it was more like three minutes.

Karissa reached the conclusion that the book was really Ms. Leonard's labor of love and she, understandably, wanted it to be perfect. No one could fault her passion; it was only the manner in which she presented herself that put the whole office on the defensive.

As if on cue, the target of Karissa's thoughts swept into the room. She always wore long, colorful clothes that made Karissa think of hippie wizards.

"Ms. Godfried," Ms. Leonard acknowledged Karissa as they sat down in the conference room.

Smiling, and motioning for the author to have a seat, Karissa replied, "Good to see you again, Ms. Leonard." She walked over and took the final copy of the book and presented it to Ms. Leonard.

As soon as Ms. Leonard felt the book in her hands, she began to cry.

Looking over at Sheila, Karissa was lost as to what she should do. She didn't normally experience this kind of reaction from authors. "I'm sorry," She rushed, "is there something wrong with the book?" She asked a, still sobbing, Ms. Leonard.

Shaking her head, no, Ms. Leonard took a few moments to compose herself before replying, "You see, I wrote this book years ago for my little boy." She looked up from the book to Karissa. "He loved the story and I felt so special for telling it to him before bed." She took a tissue that Karissa offered, and dabbed her eyes, before continuing, "He was in the Army and deployed over to Afghanistan a few years ago and was killed when his convoy came under fire." She started crying again, "I swore to myself that I would do whatever I could to get this book published so other mothers could read it to their little boys and girls." She smiled then, the tears still running down her cheeks, "I loved Dale so much."

Karissa was crying now along with Ms. Leonard. When she looked over to Sheila, she saw her assistant was dabbing tears from her own eyes too. Sitting down beside Ms. Leonard, Karissa took the author's hands, and said, "I promise that Dale would be so very proud of you for writing this book."

Squeezing her editor's hand,
Ms. Leonard said, "Thank you
Karissa, I hope so."

The meeting only lasted a few
more minutes before Ms. Leonard
left the office. She thanked the staff
and promised to be in good spirits at
the formal book release in a few
weeks.

Before she did anything else,
Karissa walked into her office and
shut the door behind her. She
needed to email lane and asked
Sheila to give her a few minutes
without being disturbed.
Unusually quiet, Sheila agreed.
Karissa sat down at her desk
and started typing…….

To: LHuff1988@email.com
From: KGodfried@HCB.com

Subject: A crazy morning

Dear Lane:

I had my final meeting with the author I've been complaining to you about for months now. It was the meeting in which I gave her the finished copy of the book. To give you a little reference, usually these meetings are celebratory, and the author is filled with excitement at the completion of their hard work. Not today. I handed Ms. Leonard her copy of the book and she broke down into tears.

I didn't know what to do at first, so I just stood there. When she finally spoke, she told me a story that blew my mind. You see, she made up the story years ago when her son was a little boy and told it to him at bedtime.

When her son grew up, he went into the Army and was deployed to Afghanistan. Sadly, he was killed there.

Not only was the story so sad, but I was slapped in the face with the reality of what you must face on a daily basis. Only, you are too kind to tell me the details of it, or you simply cannot tell me. Either way, I have to admit to you that I am scared.

This fear is deep and has consumed my mind. Are you in danger? Am I being naïve in thinking that everything will be okay? You said I could ask questions, and these are the ones that are weighing heavily on my mind today.

Truthfully, I cannot even comprehend a day without an email from you. But, I also realized that I've never heard the sound of your voice. I've never seen pictures of you as a child. I've never asked you what your biggest fears were or what you consider your biggest accomplishments to be.

Please know that I'm praying for

your continued safety. I always say it and it's always true. Be safe! I need you!
Love,
Karissa

After she sent the email to Lane, Karissa shed a few more tears. She hoped that Lane didn't think she was being hysterical or crazy in her effort to understand his situation and their relationship.

A few minutes later, Sheila came into the office, sat down across the desk from Karissa, and asked, "Are you as stunned as I am?"

By now, the whole office had heard the story, thanks to Sheila. Everyone felt awful for thinking badly about Ms. Leonard when they found out the story behind her book. The truth was that you never knew what lay beneath someone's surface unless you asked, or they revealed it.

"I sent an email to Lane, and I asked him questions that I'd avoided up until now." She looked at Sheila, and said, "You're right, I'm in love with him, and now I'm afraid to be."

Lane was about ready to go to bed, so he checked his email one last time. Normally, he didn't get an email from Karissa at this time because she was at work. He knew her schedule now and had it posted up on his wall beside his computer.

When he saw the email from her, he was smiling. The subject line was intriguing so he read the email quickly, his smile fading as her words tore through him.

She'd just exposed his biggest fear as well. Instead of starting a new email, he hit reply and started typing.

Dear Karissa:

First things first, yes, I am in danger. But, so is everyone else on this planet. Am I more likely to be injured or killed than most people, well, probably so. But, I chose this life, I chose this job, and I wouldn't have it any other way.

My biggest fear is that you will stop writing because of your fears. My biggest accomplishment so far is doing my job and doing it well. I'll make sure Terri gets some pictures of us as kids from my mom and I'll do what I can to ease your fears. I'll do whatever it takes to make us work.

I can't even comprehend a day

without hearing from you either.

The story you told me is very sad,
and one I've witnessed here. It was my
friend. It was when I was here on the
last tour. He was a good man with a
wife and baby. I do understand, to
some extent, the grief of a woman who
lost her son in a war. When you see her
again, please give her my condolences.

I'm about to hit the rack for the
night and will dream of us. I promise
you that I will be as safe as I can be
while I'm here. I'll email you again in
the morning. Have a better day.
Love,
Lane

Karissa was sending her boss
an email updating him on the
release of Ms. Leonard's book when
she saw a new message in her inbox.
When she saw it was a reply form
Lane, she clicked on it right away.

As she read his words, Karissa's fears began to ease. They didn't dissipate, but they were a little less frantic than when she sent the email to him earlier.

It was easy to see that he was thinking she was going to stop their emailing and hurt him. The thought did cross her mind, but only for a few seconds before she discounted it. She remembered the saying, "Without risk, there is no reward." She couldn't remember who said it but thinking that they were wise. She was risking the only thing she couldn't replace, her heart. If Lane broke it, well, she would be better for the experience of it. She knew that.

Picking up her phone, Karissa dialed Terri's number. When it went to voicemail, Karissa left a message saying, "This is your friend and your brother said you could score me some childhood pics of him from your parents. Make it happen." She hung up the phone and smiled.

Chapter 8

September flew by, and with it, a hot spell that made Karissa's hair frizz and her mood sour.

She would be relieved when the overly long Texas summer would settle into fall, which usually didn't happen until late October or early November.

The last few weeks were busy getting Ms. Leonard off on her book tour for The Quail With No Tail, and herself back into some semblance of down time. She'd already discussed it with her boss and decided against taking his offer of some additional vacation. She explained that she might want to take some extra time over the holidays instead if a friend could come for a visit. She failed to say that the "friend" was Lane.

The emails between her and her "friend" Lane were heating up as well. They emailed several times a day now, sometimes only sending a sentence or two if that's all they had time for. It didn't matter because it was the quality of the words, not the length that moved Karissa and made her smile.

It was is Ms. Leonard's emotional disclosure set off an avalanche of emotions within Karissa. Now, she was discussing more intimate things with Lane.

Terri was helpful and got her some pictures of Lane from his childhood. They were adorable but she could tell he was embarrassed when she told him she'd seen them.

Thinking about Lane was becoming her other full-time job and it was one that Karissa was happy to have. He made her laugh and made her think. Intellectually, he challenged her and that was something a of women she knew couldn't say about their significant others.

Her computer made the noise signaling an incoming message, so Karissa clicked on it. She smiled when she saw it was from Lane. When she opened the email, she saw it was a video file, and immediately clicked on it.

There, on the screen, was Lane. She could see he was outside and listened…….

"Karissa, hello from Afghanistan," he said and waved. "My friend, Kenston, is recording this for me so you can hear the sound of my voice. I thought it might be a nice surprise." He smiled the whole time he was talking.

Just then, Sheila came into the

room, saw the look on Karissa's face, and rounded the desk. She didn't say anything, only watched the video over Karissa's shoulder.

"So, I had to really think about what I wanted to say to you, since is the first time I've done anything like this," He winked at the camera. "So, here goes," he took a breath, and asked, "would you like to date? I know it will be a good month or so before I get back stateside but I'd like to come to Houston to see you."

Karissa was holding her hand over her mouth in awe of how sweet this man was. She nodded, even though she knew he couldn't see her do it.

"I'm not sure you've got access to software for a video, but if you do,

I'd like your answer that way so I can hear your voice too." He smiled again, "Know that I think about you all the time," He grimaced when Kenston poked his head around to the camera and yelled, "He really does."

Giggling, Karissa felt a tear slip down her cheek.

"So, I hope to hear from you soon, bye." He waved again and the video ended.

Karissa sat there, staring at the blank screen for almost a minute, not saying anything.

Sheila found her voice, and said, "Wow, he's adorable and a gentleman, I think I'm in love."

Looking up, Karissa giggled again. "Oh my Lord, Sheila, he is adorable and his voice is so......

Nodding, Sheila agreed, and said, "Yes, I know."

Finally coming out of the fog, Karissa asked her assistant, "Do we have video equipment here?"

Lane slept well the night after he sent to video to Karissa. Although annoying, Kenston was a big help and Lane promised to put in a good word for him with Terri the next time he talked to her. He told Lane that he'd finally got up the courage to email Lane's sister, but she hadn't replied yet.
The video wasn't that great

since he really had no idea what he wanted to say, but he wanted her to hear his voice and know how he felt. Reading words and hearing someone's voice were very different things. Their emails were making things more real, and he wanted to reassure Karissa that he was fully invested in their relationship.

Sure, they hadn't technically met yet, but they knew more about one another than a lot of couples Lane knew.

He knew her favorite color was blue, not just regular blue, but robin's egg blue. She hated broccoli but ate it because it was good for her. Even though she wore high heels for work, she kicked them off as soon as she sat down at her desk. She kept her hair shorter so it wouldn't get into her face when she was working out, which she tried to do three days a week.

The picture she sent him of her apartment confirmed his thoughts. It was tidy, with neutral colors, but she threw in colorful accents like pillows are a lamp that broke up the calmness. Lane imagined that was how Karissa was, calm, but with some dramatic flair thrown in to mix things up a bit.

He'd never kissed her but he knew how her lips looked when she smiled, when she was trying to be professional, and when she was being goofy since she sent him some pictures of herself over the years.

With four weeks left in their rotation, Lane found himself making plans to go to Texas, rather than Virginia, where his parents lived. He'd already told him mother, who was supportive of his decision. Terri had blabbed about him and

Karissa writing so it actually paved the way for his not visiting them.

When he woke up the next morning, one of his off-duty days, he went through his regular morning routine and checked his email. He saw one from Karissa and smiled. His smiled turned into shock when he saw the video attachment. He clicked on it and sat back in his chair to watch......

"Lane, hello" Karissa greeted him. "I'm super nervous because I've never sent a video before. My assistant slash videographer, Sheila, assures me that it's easy." She gripped her hands together in nervousness. "I would love it if you came to Texas to visit. I'm actually planning on taking some time off of work so we can spend some time together." Her cheeks flushed, and she asked, "Is that too forward?" She took a breath and went on to say, "Your video was so great, I cried. And I'd be honored to date you." She took another breath, crinkled her nose, and added, "So I guess this is it. I think about you all the time too so don't stop emailing or I'm pretty sure I'll fall to pieces." She waved at him, and closed with, "Bye."

Sitting in his chair, Lane smiled like a kid on Christmas morning. Oh, she was even more beautiful when she talked. Her nervousness was apparent, but that only made her look more beautiful.

He thought about the video for a few more minutes, then started his email to her.

To: KGodfried@HCB.com
From: LHuff1988@email.com
Subject: Your video was great!

Dear Karissa:

I'm sure you can guess that I'm smiling pretty big now. You are gorgeous, and I hope I don't embarrass you but it's the God's honest truth.

I won't stop writing. Nothing could make me stop. I feel like we're both sort of skirting around the words, but I know in my heart that we're both thinking them. I won't say them in a mere email or video, I'll wait to see you to tell you.

Everyone here is starting to get antsy because our rotation date is about four weeks out. I know that's close to Halloween so maybe we can decorate together. Did I mention that my family decorates for every single holiday, no exceptions!

I see us sitting by the door, waiting for trick-or-treaters to come by. Is that too cheesy? I love the holidays and I love to celebrate.

What do you do for the holidays? I guess I never asked that. Do you decorate or have specific traditions you follow? Let me know.

Well, I'm off to breakfast. I'll say hi to Kenston for you. He still hasn't heard from Terri so he's being a big baby and pouting. I supposed I'd be the exact same way if I didn't hear from you so I really should be more empathetic to his issue. Maybe you could put in a good word with Terri? After all, she did practically force you to write me, and I hope it's turning out as well for you as it is for me.

"I'll write later today. We're off duty so it will be a relaxing day. The guys were talking about a dart marathon. We'll see how I do.

Love,
Lane

Lane sent off the email, grabbed his cover, and was going out the door to the mess tent when he heard the muster announcement.

Karissa read Lane's email the next morning and smiled. She was in bed since it was Saturday and was determined to follow his orders to relax and take care of herself.

So far, Ms. Leonard's book was doing even better than the publishing house anticipated and it made Karissa proud to be a part of the process.

She'd earned a day of leisure and intended on using it to plan some activities for her and Lane to do while he was here.

There were still a few logistical

questions she had, like was he planning on staying at her apartment with her?

She wanted him to stay at her place, but she wasn't sure how to ask him without it sounding needy. Maybe he'd feel more comfortable at Terri's place? She made a mental note to ask Terri about it the next time they got together.

Looking at her laptop, Karissa got out a paper and pen and started making a list of things happening in Houston around Halloween.

Chapter 9

Lane came out of the meeting and was pissed. He wasn't the only one, and if he asked around, he was sure that everyone else felt the same way. Their tour was being extended and no one could tell them for how long.

There was also some heightened activity in the area that led intelligence to believe there would be an uptake on the skirmishes with the local terrorist-related groups. So, not only were they being forced to stay longer, but they were also fairly certain that they would have encounters with the people who didn't want them here. Great!

"Can you believe this bullsh…," Kenston started to say, but stopped when he saw the look on Lane's face. "Sorry," He mumbled, and headed back towards his own room.

When Lane finally got back to his own room, he sat down and looked at pictures of Karissa he put on a slide show on his laptop. Sitting there, he just watched the pictures as they flashed on the screen. He wasn't sure what to say to her. Deciding to enlist the help of his sister, Lane sent an email to Terri asking for advice.

Karissa was shocked that there was no email from Lane the next morning. Maybe he was too busy? But he always sent one, so not getting one just started her day off sadly.

A few hours later, her phone

rang. She smiled when she saw it was Terri and said, "Hello there," with a smile.

Terri didn't really know what she was going to say and didn't relish the thought that she was the go-between for her brother and Karissa. "Uh, I called because Lane asked me to," She admitted.

The sound of her friend's voice sent a chill up Karissa's spine. "What's wrong?" She asked, the bubble of worry exploding in her chest.

"Nothing," Terri said quickly. "He just got some new and didn't know how to tell you. Their deployment has been extended, and they don't know how long. Nobody gave them dates and everyone is pissed off. He wanted you to hear it from me instead of through email." She wasn't any good at sugar coating and didn't want to anyway.

Listening to her friend, Karissa understood what Terri was saying. What she couldn't understand was how Lane thought hearing the news from his sister would be any easier than hearing it from him. "Okay, I'll email him and tell him you told me."

"He's scared," Terri explained. "He's afraid that with you not having a lot of experience with the military and how they operate, that you'll decide this being apart thing isn't worth it."

A feeling of anger worked its way up Karissa's body. She wasn't angry with Terri, but she was upset with Lane for thinking she couldn't handle this. "Terri, I'll let him know you did your job," she said, but couldn't help the feeling of anger that tinged the words.

After hanging up with Terri, Karissa immediately pulled up her email and began typing……..

To: LHuff1988@email.com
From: KGodfried@HCB.com
Subject: I'm actually mad.

Dear Lane,
        I just received a call from Terri saying that your deployment has been extended. Logically, I realize that you were trying to shield me from bad news, but having your sister call me? I would have taken it far better had it been you who emailed me the

information.

Haven't we been writing and emailing for months now and developing a relationship of trust and understanding? If that's the case, then all information should come straight from you, not through a filter you deem necessary.

It seems that you don't think I'm strong enough to handle this. Well, I am. I handle million-dollar book deals, crazy artistic people, and manage just fine so this setback isn't going to break me.

It was hurtful to not have an email to read this morning, by the way. If you're afraid to proceed, let me know. I would understand, but I won't risk my heart for someone who doesn't look at me as his equal.

If I'm not being clear about anything, please let me know.
Be Safe!

Karissa

Lane returned from his morning duty and was beat. There was a little scuffle with some rather unfriendly people as their convoy was going through a nearby city, but everyone made it back and that's what counted.

He got some lunch and went to check his email. All morning his gut was churning with nerves over what Terri suggested. He didn't know how to do this the "right" way. He only knew that he didn't want Karissa to be hurt.

After just reading the subject line, Lane knew he'd made a mistake. As he read the paragraphs, his chest ached. Oh boy did he make a mistake.

Not knowing what to do now, Lane left his room and walked

down the hall to a friend of his, Tony Walker's, room. He knocked and waited for his friend to say, "come in," before opening the door. Sitting down in an empty folding chair, Lane asked, "You've been married a while now, right?"

Tony smiled and nodded.

Then Lane asked, "What do you do when you realize you screwed up?"

Sitting back in another folding chair, Tony thought about the question for a few moments, before saying, "Well, there's sort of a sliding scale for these things," he looked serious, "if it was a minor infraction, flowers are good, mid-way to blow up, then definitely jewelry, and something akin to the sinking of the Titanic, well, you might never recover. What did you do?" He asked Lane, a half-smile on his face.

Lane launched into the explanation of how he relayed the news, via his sister, to Karissa about the change in their rotation date. He also divulged that his sister was the one who suggested she be the one to call Karissa and let her know.

His eyebrows raised, Tony waited for Lane to finish the story, before saying, "Well, this sounds like a first argument, if I'm understanding things, right?"

Lane nodded.

Tony continued on, saying, "Then you have to do two things,

number one, don't be an idiot. Women hate that, and when we try to "shield" them, or "spare" them, they feel like we think they can't handle things." He clapped his friend on the shoulder, and told him, "Number two, I'd categorize this as a medium sized infraction so maybe flower and a dinner or something." He thought for a second, and asked, "You said she was friends with your sister, right?"

Again, Lane nodded.

Tony suggested, "Then give them a girls' night out on you."

A few minutes later, Lane was back in his room, searching for flower delivery services in Houston. He knew where Karissa's office was because he googled it not long after they started emailing back and forth. Luckily, he found a shop that did same day service but realized he didn't know what her favorite flower was. Luckily the website had some suggestions and pictures.

After another twenty aggravating minutes of looking at flower arrangements, and cringing at the cost, Lane made his selection and put in his credit card information.

Once he was done with that, he emailed Terri to give you a "good email talking to" and then asked what restaurant she and Karissa liked to go to.

When parts one and two of his plan were complete, Lane sat down and started an email to Karissa. He was determined to mend things between them.

To: KGodfried@HCB.com
From: LHuff@email.com
Subject: Okay, I realize I messed up.

Dear Karissa:

As soon as I saw the subject line in your last email, I realized I made a mistake. You're right, I shouldn't keep things from you. In my heart, I wanted to make the news less hurtful and instead, I hurt you. There are no words to express how sorry I am.

We're in this together, and therefore, all further information will go through you first. I ended up talking to a friend of mine who has been married a while. I hold me I wasn't being smart (but he used a bit more colorful language) and explained that women don't like to be left out of anything regarding their relationship. Duly noted! I am now more aware of what I should be doing, which is to make sure that you are the first person to know what's going on.

I swear to you that my heart led me in this action, and I can't promise that I won't have feelings of wanting to protect you from any unpleasantness, but I will be respectful enough to understand that you need to hear it from me and me alone.

Please forgive me?

Love,

Lane

Lane sent off the email and prayed that Karissa was as forgiving as she was talented and beautiful.

And he also knew he couldn't be an idiot, even if it was motivated by love.

Chapter 10

The next day, flowers arrived for Karissa. And not just any flowers either, but a beautiful, not to mention, huge, bouquet that practically hid the delivery guy behind it.

Sheila walked beside him, as he entered Karissa's office, a sly grin on her face.

Accepting the flowers, Karissa was afraid she'd drop the vase, it was so heavy. She could see her curious co-workers looking over their computers toward her office.

Sheila commented, "If you don't put them down and read the card, I'm going to grab it from you."

Smiling, Karissa placed the

vase on the small conference table in her office. The bouquet was almost the same width as the tabletop. She pulled out the card, smelling the beautiful aroma drifting from the flowers.

Reading it quietly at first, Karissa smiled. She read it out loud to Sheila before her assistant had a meltdown. "Karissa, a married friend of mine advised me to send flowers first, and then to grovel. I'm so sorry. Love, Lane."

As she looked from the bouquet, to Sheila, and back again, Karissa knew he was forgiven and that he meant it. She didn't comment further, only stared at the beautiful arrangement and soaked up the scintillating aroma.

"So, let me get this straight," Sheila commented, "this guy is gorgeous, sweet, romantic, and is so into you that he finds a way to send this," she pointed to the flowers, "to you from Afghanistan."

Giving Sheila a dry look, and feeling a bit cheeky, she said, "Well the flowers aren't from Afghanistan." At the look her assistant gave her, Karissa added, "Well, when you put it that way, I feel stupid."

Laughing, Sheila gave her boss a hug, and followed up with, "I suggest you snag that man as fast as you can," and left the office.

A few minutes later, Karissa was still standing in the middle of her office, staring at the bouquet. Her whole office smelled like a spring garden in bloom. When she finally snapped out of her "flower trance," she walked over to her desk and sat down to write an email to Lane.

As soon as she opened her email, she saw there was one there from Lane already, so she clicked on it to read what he said. He apologized again for upsetting her and she did firmly believe he regretted the way he handled the first real hurdle in their relationship. She began typing……..

To: LHuff1988@email.com
From: KGodfried@HCB.com
Subject: The flowers are amazing!!!!!!

Dear Lane,
    Imagine my shock when this enormous flower arrangement shows up in my office accompanied by a very touching note. I just read your most

recent email and I accept your apology. I guess we're both just trying to navigate waters we've never been in before.

Please tell your married friend that he is very knowledgeable about his advice. That means either he gets in trouble a lot, or that he's a quick study. Either way, Bravo!

You should see all the ladies here in our office. They are practically drooling over this beautiful bouquet. I'm not normally snooty and brag, but this is truly gorgeous. You shouldn't have, but secretly, I'm so glad you did. I'm going to take a picture and send it to Terri and tell her how wonderful her brother is being.

Back to the subject at hand, I agree, we need to let one another know things. I know you were planning on spending Halloween here, and sure, I'm disappointed that isn't going to happen, but I'd rather have you show up later, and safe.

I understand that this is a day-by-day process. I'm willing to wait, Lane, as long as is necessary, if it means we can finally meet in person and spend some time together.

Sure, there are things we need to work out, but I'm confident we'll work them out together.
Be Safe!
Love,
Karissa

After sending off her email, Karissa noticed that she was due to join a meeting with a new author the company was bringing on. She gave the beautiful flowers one last glance before getting up and leaving her office.

Lane came in from another

protection detail and was dirty from all the dust flying. They practically raced through the city to beat a dust storm and they didn't quite make it before the high winds were blowing everything, including their vehicles, around.

He showered and then decided to skip eating dinner because he was just too tired. Before he knew it, he was looking at his email and hoping for a reply from Karissa.

Sure enough, there was an email there and Lane woke up from the excitement of seeing it. She forgave him, thank goodness. He owed Tony a big thank you.

His stomach growled and he realized that he needed to eat. He owed it to Karissa to stay healthy and safe. Closing his laptop, he went to the mess tent, a huge smile on his face.

When he got back to his room after eating, he decided he wanted to send an email to Karissa, so she had one when she woke up.

He started typing…….

To: KGodfried@HCB.com
From: LHuff1988@email.com
Subject: I'm relieved

Dear Karissa:

This email will be short, sorry. We just got back a little bit ago and I'm beat so I'm off to bed. I just wanted to let you know I got your email.

I'm glad you love the flowers, although their beauty is dwarfed by yours.

I hope you had sweet dreams because I know I will. I'll email you as soon as I wake up in the morning.

Love,
Lane

Closing his laptop, Lane smiled and crawled into his cot. He was asleep within two minutes and his dreams were filled with Karissa.

Karissa woke up refreshed and wasn't sure why. She'd gotten to bed later than usual the night before and was a little down that there wasn't another email from Lane. She had to take into consideration the time difference, but it was tough.

After her meeting with the new author, who was fantastic, she had dinner with an old friend from college who happened to be in town. She ended up finding out a few very interesting things too. Her friend, Rita, had a friend who was married to a Marine so promised to get the two women connected. She told Karissa that it would be good to speak to someone who actually did know what she was going through. It might help her understand Lane and the way he reacted to the change in plans.

As soon as she got home from dinner, she texted Rita's friend, Jasmine, and introduced herself.

Within minutes, the two women were on a phone call and finally hung up an hour later.

Karissa felt like her eyes were now opened up to what life with a Marine might be like. Nothing was certain, after all, he may not feel the same way she did.

October came into Texas and was scarier than Halloween. There was a stream of thunderstorms that tore through the area, dropping torrential rains and causing a lot of flooding in the Houston area.

Karissa wasn't even able to drive to work for a few days.

Her boss just told everyone to stay home and stay safe.

She was lucky because her building was in a higher area and didn't get the horrible flooding that other parts of Houston did.

The only downside was the power was sketchy, going on and off, a couple of times a day. She was able to get an email out to Lane during one of the "on" times and explained what was going on and why there may be a gap in her emails to him.

Being cooped up in her apartment gave Karissa some good time to think. She lit candles at night instead of turning on lights. It gave the rooms a soft glow and made her think of Lane. Would he like her apartment? From the pictures she'd sent him, he wrote that he did, but pictures were different than real life.

Going down that mental railroad track, Karissa's mind wondered if he would even like her when they met in person. Sure, he said the pictures and video were great, calling her gorgeous, but what if they met and he didn't really think she looked pretty?

At the end of her second day home, she gave herself an honest pep talk. She didn't need to wonder about Lane's thoughts because he would tell her about them when they met.

The power currently on, Karissa quickly booted up her laptop and sent him an email.....

To: LHuff1988@email.com
From: KGodfried@HCB.com

Subject: It's too quiet.

Dear Lane:

With the storms making the power temperamental, I decided to write this to you quickly before I went to bed.

Having two days, at home and by myself, is too much time to think. I've started to worry about whether or not you'll think my apartment looks nice or whether you'll still think I'm pretty. (Not that I would say that about myself, but who am I to dispute your opinion.)

Now I've managed to shake off my doubts and know that whatever happens when we finally meet, it will all be worth it. The last months have made me realize how lonely I've been and, honestly, a little ashamed that I didn't even notice how cut off from life I allowed myself to get.

You woke me up out of a trance of

mere existence and I'm so grateful to you for that. Granted, my life revolved around work, and you, so I'm not entirely sure I've changed my habits, but my eyes have been opened and that's half the battle.

When we are finally together, let's just take some time to be quiet. I know that probably sounds like a strange request but being quiet with someone is important. You need to know if that person is someone who you can be quiet with or if you feel like you need to fill up the time.

For some reason, I think being quiet with you will be more exciting than most of the conversations I have on any given day.

I'm finally going to bed but know I'm thinking of you.

Love,

Karissa

Chapter 11

Lane was sitting in his room when he heard his email go off. Today he was feeling particularly down because his company's original departure date was two days earlier, and right now, he would've been in Houston, with Karissa.

Some of the guys were feeling the same way and no one could blame them. They were given orders and most people knew that plans could change.

Karissa's emails were bright spots in his days, explaining things about her life to him. She met another Marine's wife a few weeks earlier and told Lane that they'd been talking. She told him that it gave her new insight into his life, and she appreciated the new perspective.

All Lane wanted to appreciate, was Karissa.

Tomorrow was a big day for his command. A couple of VIP's were flying in, and it was his squad's job to provide security for them while here. Depending on the itinerary, it could get tricky, but Lane trusted his men and their abilities.

There was a knock on the door, and Kenston came in without waiting for him to say anything.

Looking at his friend, Kenston shook his head. "Stop being a baby, Huff," he told Lane. "Focus on what you're going to do when you get there, not what you're missing right now."

Even knowing his friend was right, it was still tough. "Wise words," he said to Kenston.

"Not my words exactly," Kenston said and shrugged. He turned around and left Lane's room as quickly as he came in.

Deciding to go along with the advice, Lane sat down at his computer and started an email to Karissa.......

To: KGodfried@HCB.com
From: LHuff1988@email.com
Subject: I'm leaving the pity party now.

Dear Karissa:
    I had an interesting visit from Kenston a few minutes ago. Surprisingly, he had some nice words of wisdom for me. I decided to quit worrying about what we were missing and focus more on what we should do

when we finally meet.

I'd like to take you out to a nice restaurant, preferably not someplace sandy, and show you that I was raised with manners.

I picture you in a beautiful dress, in your favorite color of blue, and us holding hands.

As you can read, I'm being old-fashioned here and not discussing anything further than that at this time.

I think it's important to me that we take this slowly. As you said, in person is different than sending letters or emails. I think it will be better, but I can see your point.

I've also been doing some research about Houston and the surrounding areas. Not that you won't have plans, because you've told me you're a natural "planner," but I'd like to see Galveston. I've never been to the Gulf of Mexico, and I think it would be cool. Have you gone there a lot?

My parents emailed me and asked if I'm coming to Virginia to see them. Thanks to Terri, they know we've been writing. (I think she did it to divert attention from herself.) My mother, Natalie, wanted me to extend an invitation for you to join me.

Not sure if you want to jump right into the family thing, I'm game if you are but we've been talking about going slow.

We have some additional duties over the next couple of days, so PLEASE don't feel upset if I don't write as much. It certainly won't be for lack of wanting to.

Please take care and send me pictures of your Halloween decorations.
Love,
Lane

Karissa woke up and stretched.

The temp here was only supposed to be in the sixties today so she was excited to get a taste of fall.

Pulling out her laptop, she opened it up.

Halloween was in a couple of days, so she asked for a few days off of work to decorate. With the success of the books she worked on this year, her boss was more than happy to oblige.

She saw the email from Lane in her inbox first. Her eyes automatically looked for it in her inbox now. She read the email and felt warm with love. The ending sentences made her a little sad, but he said maybe, so it may not affect their emails at all.

Smiling, Karissa got out of bed and headed to the kitchen to start breakfast.

An hour later, she was knee deep in Halloween decorations. She ordered them when she thought Lane would be here to help her. "Regretting that now, aren't you?" she asked herself out loud.

Pushing up her sleeves, she decided there was no point in procrastinating, and got to work.

Hours later, Karissa stood back and enjoyed her efforts.

There was a good mix of creepy and fun, at least in her opinion. Picking up her phone, she started snapping pictures to email to Lane.

She also sent the pictures to Terri with a text......

Where's your brother when I need him?

A few minutes later Terri texted her back......

Looks good, you don't need him. You handled it just fine on your own.

Karissa replied......

I did, didn't I?

Working the rest of the day on decorating her front door, Karissa was in a good mood. She even donated some of her leftover decorations to a family down the hall, which made her feel better. It wasn't often that she took some time off of work, and she realized she needed it.

After a dinner that consisted of a salad and a small bowl of frozen yogurt, Karissa smiled. She couldn't very well deny herself the little pleasures life afforded.

She sat down in front of the television, her laptop on her lap, and composed an email to Lane……

To: LHuff1988@email.com
From: KGodfried@HCB.com
Subject: I rock Halloween decorations!

Dear Lane:

I sort of failed to mention to you that when you first suggested you might be here for Halloween, that I ordered a ton of decorations. Well, not a wise move since I had enough to decorate two apartments. I gave my leftover decorations to a family down the hall with kids old enough to help decorate and appreciate the fun of it.

It was fun, but it would have been more fun if you were here. I'm not trying to make you feel guilty, just making an honest observation. I sent the pictures to you and to Terri. She thought I did a great job. Please confirm that you got the pictures since you were the one who asked for them in the first place.

Also, I requested today and tomorrow off of work. I have to admit that you were right, I needed the time off to destress and relax. When you go a hundred miles an hour workwise, it's a bit difficult to slow down. I'll make a more concerted effort to do it though, I promise.

My parents called me and asked about my plans for Christmas. Since you're not sure when you'll be stateside, I went ahead and committed to joining them in California from Christmas to New Year's.

They live in a small town in Central California. I'm not sure if I told you that already. It's almost rustic but I love the feel of it when I'm there. Everyone knows everyone else, and they decorate like crazy for the holidays. Terri mentioned that she had plans with your parents in Virginia over that time too.

I'm honestly not sure if it's okay to talk about this with you. Does it hurt your feelings? Do you feel like we're leaving you out? I want to understand so please tell me.

I will keep you posted on how many Trick-or-Treaters come to my door. We usually have a good turnout because there are a lot of families in the building.

The most difficult part of today was thinking of us together. I just kept thinking, 'Would Lane like this? Or Would Lane do that?' Is that weird? Every single day I think about you, but I think, up until now, it was more about the idea of you and now it's more real. I hope that makes some sense to you.

How is Kenston? Is he still teasing you about writing to me? Please tell him I said hello and that if he wanted to be your cameraman again, I'd appreciate it.

For some reason, unknown to me, I realized that I've never asked you when your birthday was. Mine is May 5th. Again, don't know why I threw that little tidbit in there, but there you have it.

Be safe over there, I really want to see you.

Love,
Karissa

Shutting the laptop, Karissa sat on the sofa for a while. She looked at the tv, but didn't have a clue what was on it. She only saw Lane.

Chapter 12

As October left and November moved in, Lane found himself working more and more. Some of the personnel not attached to his group, were rotating out, so Lane's platoon was expected to pick up the slack until the replacements were in place.

He was dog tired most days, and only managed to get a few sentences in an email to Karissa. But, he refused to go a day without sending her an email, even if they were short. It was important to him that she know how committed he was to her and their relationship.

She did send him a trick-or-treaters count, and it was rather impressive. It made him sad to know he missed it. They were only three weeks out from Thanksgiving and there was still no word on when they would be rotating out. There was some issue with the incoming company.

Lane tried daily to reassure Karissa that he was okay, and she should share her plans with him. It made him feel more connected to know what was going on in her daily life.

Terri promised to keep him updated as well, but Lane suspected something was going on with his sister. She didn't email him nearly as much as she did before, and now, her emails were short.

If he wasn't so beat, he'd ask, but as it was, all of his left-over energy was focused on Karissa.

They heard some news about the incoming troops being cleared in the next week or two so things were hopefully going to settle down.

His squad was going out on

patrol in a few hours, and he needed to rest, or we wouldn't be of much use to them.

Closing his eyes, Lane smiled as Karissa's face filled his mind. Her smile lulled him into sleep.

Three hours later, Lane's platoon was out on patrol. Each group was assigned a time to patrol the perimeter of the base. It wasn't for too long, but there was some suspected unfriendly activity reported.

Lane was in the first Humvee, along with his driver, gunman, and lookout.

They were just turned around a corner of a building when the gunfire started.

"Down," Lane shouted to the men in the back, then told the

driver, "get us out of here."

Luckily, the Sergeant driving was good and got them out of the area and back onto the base quickly.

Lane was on the radio reporting the incident as they drove back to the parking area for their unit.

Kenston ran out and started asking questions as soon as they got out of the vehicle.

Lane shook his head at his friend's antics. It was only when the Sgt. gave him an odd look that Lane felt the twinge in his left arm. When he looked down, he saw the blood stain spreading across his sleeve.

"Holy Crap," The gunman yelled and followed with, "medic!"

Before Lane could even tell them he was fine to walk, he found himself on a stretcher and being rushed over to the base hospital.

A nurse cut away his sleeve to check the wound first.

The doctor followed a couple of minutes later, and checked it, before saying, "Looks like a through and through," he glanced up at Lane and smiled, "you were lucky."

Instead of feeling upset or scared, Lane started to laugh. When the nurse gave him a questioning look, Lane told her, "Good thing, if it was worse, my girlfriend would kill me."

Laughing at the comment, the medical staff understood how odd it would sound in any other place but a combat zone.

Within the hour, he was

stitched up and sent to his CO to be debriefed.

Karissa was back to work the following week, and in a meeting with her newest author when Sheila came into the conference room.

"Uh, excuse me, Ms. Godfried, you have a phone call," Sheila said in a formal tone.

Two things that Karissa knew, one; Sheila never referred to her directly as Ms. Godfried, and two; Sheila would never interrupt a meeting unless it was important.

Looking at the author, Ms. Rathbone, Karissa told her, "If you'll excuse me for just a minute or two," and got up to follow Sheila out of the conference room.

When they were in the hallway, and headed for Karissa's office, Sheila leaned over and said, "Terri is on the phone. She called the office number, not your personal cell, and she sounds really upset."

Stepping up her pace, Karissa went into her office, allowing Sheila to close the door behind her, and picked up the phone. She asked Terri, "What's wrong?"

Terri was crying. She wasn't sure if she was crying because she was mad at her brother or mad at the person who shot him, or mad that she was crying. "Lane was shot," she choked out in response to Karissa's question. Then she rushed to say, "In the arm, and he's okay."

Karissa literally felt her heart

stop beating in her chest for a few moments. "Is he still there?" She asked, trying to remain calm on the outside while feeling hysterical on the inside.

Still crying, but her voice more understandable, Terri answered, "Yes, they said it was minor. Kenston emailed me as soon as they took Lane to the hospital, so I knew before my parents did. The doctors had Lane call Mom and Dad from the hospital to confirm that he was okay."

A tear slipped down Karissa's cheek. She wasn't sure if it was relief or hurt. It was understandable that Lane would call his parents because they were his next of kin, but it still stung to know that she wouldn't be contacted if anything were to happen to him. That hadn't occurred to her before.

Again, she found herself being slapped in the face, and in the heart, with the realization of what their situation was. "But he's okay?" She asked Terri, trying to calm herself down.

"Yes," Terri replied, and sniffled before adding, "Kenston said that Lane kept telling him to call me so I could let you know. He didn't want you to wonder if he couldn't send you an email."

Terri's words helped soothe Karissa's hurt. He was thinking about her, even when he was hurt. "I'll email him right away and let him know you told me. Thanks for calling me, Terri. Let's have dinner at my place tonight, okay? We'll order in Chinese and laugh and cry together."

Smiling through her tears, Terri told her friend, "Sounds wonderful, I'll see you about five and I'll bring the wine."

Karissa hung up the phone and slumped down into her desk chair.

Sheila came into her office immediately and asked, "Is everything okay?"

After she took a deep breath, Karissa was able to respond, and said, "He was shot in the arm, but I guess it's not serious."

Her hand over her chest, Sheila walked over and put her other hand on Karissa's shoulder, before asking,

"Do you want me to reschedule your day so you can go home?"

Karissa quickly shook her head, no. "I need to be here, and distracted, so I don't overthink this."

Sheila remained where she was until her boss was out of the office and headed back to her meeting. Then she returned to her desk, determined to keep Karissa as distracted as possible when she came out of her meeting.

Lane was barking at Kenston, "Just do it, will you?"

Rolling his eyes, Kenston turned on Lane's laptop, before saying, "This feels weird, bro."

Frustrated, Lane sighed, and said, "All I'm asking you to do is type a darn email, Kenston, not read them all and dissect my romantic life." His patience was non-existent since he refused to take any more pain medication and his arm was throbbing like crazy.

Sighing, Kenston replied, "Fine," and sat down in the chair to open up Lane's email. "There's one in your inbox from Karissa," He told his friend, and asked, "Do you want me to read it to you?"

Lane nodded and closed his eyes, willing the pain in his arm to at least settle down a bit.

Kenston read aloud.......

Dear Lane:

You just couldn't keep out of trouble, could you? I hope that made you laugh since I realized this was either a laugh or cry kind of situation.

Terri called me as soon as she found out and was pretty upset. I tried to remain calm, but the truth is, I was petrified. I need you to reassure me that you are truly okay. I could barely sleep last night thinking of you in pain. I wish I was there to ease it for you.

Terri came over last night and we ordered in Chinese food and talked about whether we thought you were brave or ridiculous. Finally, after two glasses of wine each, we decided you were most definitely brave.

I've heard that women dig scars too so I can't wait to see that if it's true.

So, here it is, I love you. I didn't want to write it in some email, but, like you said, you learn to be very open when faced with these things. If you

don't return the sentiment, I
understand, but I wanted you to know
how I felt.
Be safe, PLEASE!
Love,
Karissa

Without missing a beat,
Kenston piped up with, "Not
looking into your love life, hey?"

All Lane could do was laugh.
Karissa was right, it was a laugh or
cry kind of situation and the fact
that she wrote she loved him told
him it was going to be just fine.

Chapter 13

Lane was on light duty for the next couple of weeks until they could reassess the damage, if any, to his arm. The doctor was pretty sure the bullet damaged some muscle, but no nerves seemed to be affected. They would know more when he was out of the arm sling and tested for mobility.

The worst part was trying to send emails to Karissa. With only one working hand, it literally took him an hour to type up and send out a few paragraphs. Not that the time at the computer was the issue, he was pretty much confined to his bunk room these days. But, with that confinement, he was thinking about waiting to leave, and knowing he couldn't do anything to make the time pass faster.

To her credit, Karissa's emails

were light-hearted. He found out that a couple of the books she edited hit some literary milestones in sales and she was really making a name for herself.

Lane was proud of her and wanted to be there with her to share in the excitement of her accomplishments.

Thanksgiving was only ten days away now and he knew Terri was going to be with Karissa since neither was going home to see family until Christmas. There was some solace in knowing his sister would be with Karissa and she wouldn't be alone.

Kenston poked his head into Lane's room, and asked, "Hey, you doing okay?"

Turning around his office chair

to face his friend, Lane answered,
"Yeah, I'm fine."

Not believing his friend,
Kenston stepped into the room.
"Well, that's really convincing," he
retorted sarcastically.

Lane rubbed his hand over his
face. "I'm sorry man, I'm just
feeling sorry for myself."

"It's understandable," Kenston
nodded, "but remember, you're
walking out of here and some of our
friends didn't." His tone was
somber.

It was a rare thing when Lane's
friend was so serious, and he was
exactly right. "Thanks," Lane said to
him. He realized he had to leave his
pity party and ASAP. "Let's go see

if there's some food in the mess hall," He commented as he stood up.

Smiling again, Kenston stepped back to Lane could walk ahead of him. "Sounds like a plan."

Karissa was wandering down the aisle at the grocery store when she saw the mistletoe display. A smile traveled across her lips when she thought of making sure she had some on hand when Lane was able to come home.

She stopped, her smile fading as she processed what she just said.

"Home," She whispered out loud, and realized that she was already making a place for Lane in her life here in Houston.

As she started walking with

her cart again, Karissa's heart felt a little lighter. The worry she'd been lugging around since she found out Lane had been shot was lifting off her chest.

When she was back home and unloading her bags, she shook her head seeing that she'd bought more groceries than necessary. It was okay because she could invite Terri over for dinner again and this time it wouldn't be for a worry party about Lane.

Grabbing her laptop, Karissa sat down to write an email to Lane……

To: LHuff1988@email.com
From: KGodfried@HCB.com
Subject: How do you feel about mistletoe?

Dear Lane:

I was walking through the grocery story this evening after work and saw a display of mistletoe. Of course, my thoughts spun around to you and I had to keep myself from buying bunches of the stuff and placing all around my apartment for when you get here. Since we're not sure when you'll be leaving for the states, I decided to wait. It did make me smile though, knowing that at some point you will be here with me and we'll make it a point to get some for sure.

I hope my talk isn't embarrassing you. I know we've tried to steer away from anything really intimate, and that's what I've loved about our relationship. I never once felt pressured about anything like that.

As long as I'm going down that road, I was wondering where you'd like to stay with while you're here. I would understand if you wanted to stay with Terri, but there is always room at my place for you too. Do I sound crazy for talking about this now? My sofa is very comfortable.

Maybe it's because it's the holiday season, but I find myself crying at the commercials that are on television. It's insane to cry over a tissue or greeting card commercial, but there I am, grabbing the tissues and sniffling. Not a very lovely picture, I know.

Well, I should get off to bed. I have a busy day and will be attending the awards ceremony I told you about. I was shocked when she asked me to accompany her as her plus one. Ms. Leonard has proven to be a very nice lady and has been generous with her praise of the publishing firm.

I miss you! It seems a little strange to say still, but it's completely true. You've managed to sneak right into my heart....very covert-like, I might add. ☐
Be safe!!!!
Love,
Karissa

Karissa called Terri as soon as she sent Lane's email to him and they made a date for dinner the following week. When she hung up though, she thought there was something going on that Terri wasn't telling her. There needed to be an interrogation when Terri came over for dinner.

The next evening was an exercise in managing chaos. Karissa's firm made sure that she got off early to give her enough time to get her hair and makeup done for the awards ceremony. They also provided an expense account to buy her gown for her.

The Quail With No Tail was a literary hit with the critics and readers. Ms. Leonard was being honored this evening and asked Karissa to come along with her.

Flattered was an understatement for how Karissa felt. Most editors didn't really see this side of the book releasing process. They were more of the "behind the scenes" at the development process. Her firm had already told her she had a pick of authors so this was just an amazing bonus.

The limousine picked Karissa up first then went to pick up Ms. Leonard at her home.

When she saw the author come out and get into the car, Karissa's jaw dropped. She looked stunning.

With a dry look, Ms. Leonard commented, "Close your mouth dear, I know I look like an alien."

Giggling, Karissa shook her head no to deny the comment. "On the contrary," she said honestly, you look stunning."

"So do you," Ms. Leonard said. "I think we'll show them we're not to be trifled with this evening."

They made small talk on the way to the gala and were helped out of the limousine by an usher for the event.

It was a local even for the Houston area and, with Ms.

Leonard receiving an honor, they were treated like VIP's.

Karissa wasn't expecting so many people to be in attendance so she was more than a little nervous as they made their way up the stairs to the ballroom.

Everyone was finding their seats for the dinner portion of the evening and Karissa made sure to stick close to Ms. Leonard as they wound their way around tables to find theirs.

Once they were seated, Karissa looked around the room. It was just beautiful and she thought of the story of Cinderella. She couldn't help it if she compared things to children's literature, it was a habit.

"Why are you smiling like that?" Ms. Leonard leaned over and asked her. "Is there a special man in your life? I find that a man is about the only thing that puts that kind of smile on a woman's face."

Trying not to laugh, Karissa replied, "Actually, I was smiling because I compared the room to something out of Cinderella, but yes, there is a special man in my life."

The emcee walked up to the podium on the stage and started to speak so Ms. Leonard kept any comments she wanted to make to herself.

During the dinner, everyone chatted at their table. Karissa was impressed by the attendee list for the evening and even the group at their table was very accomplished.

When Karissa mentioned that she was an editor who worked on Ms. Leonard's book, there were a few raised eyebrows, followed by questions.

The conversation flowed easily amount their group and everyone reluctantly quieted when the emcee returned to the podium to start the award portion of the evening.

When Ms. Leonard's name was announced, she got up and made her way up onto the stage. "Thank you," she spoke when she got to the microphone. Looking at the award for a few moments, she continued, "This book was a true labor of love, and I dedicate it to my son, Dale, and my editor, Karissa. They were the two people in the whole world who believed in my far more than I believed in myself."

As Ms. Leonard was escorted off the stage, Karissa looked down at her hands and tried to hold back the tears.

Later, when Ms. Leonard came back to their table, she Karissa a tight squeeze and whispered, "Thank you," into her ear.

Smiling, Karissa replied, "Thank you."

"Let's get a picture so you can send to your special man," Ms. Leonard said with a wink. She handed her phone to another person at their table and asked them to take a quick photo.

Chapter 14

Lane was eating his dinner in his room. The sling came off just after Thanksgiving and felt a lot better. It sucked having to depend on others for simple things.

The doctor told him, again, that he was lucky. His arm seemed to be working well and there was no damage that looked long term. He gave Lane specific strengthening exercises to help him rebuild his muscle tone in that arm, and he followed the orders tot the letter. He wanted to get better as fast as possible.

Once he got the picture of Karissa and her author at the awards ceremony, he printed it out and framed it for his desk. She was stunning, all decked out for the occasion.

Seeing her was great, but it

made him that much more excited
to see her in person.

Luckily, his CO started putting
him into the duty rotations again so
time passed much faster with things
to do.

His new mission was to hound
his sister to figure out what Karissa
wanted for Christmas. His sister
was being her usual, bratty self and
didn't get back to him although he'd
asked her multiple times in his
emails.

Thank goodness for internet
shopping because he could at least
get something to her for Christmas if
necessary.

It was early December now and
he was really getting restless. They
were six weeks past their original
rotation date and although there
were rumors, nothing was
confirmed yet. Mostly, Lane

assumed it was the guys trying to keep their morale up.

Almost finished with his dinner, Lane was about to open up his laptop to write an email to Karissa when there was a knock, and Kenston poked his head into the room.

"Hey," Kenston smiled at Lane, "meeting in the mess hall I five minutes."

Although Lane wanted to hope this was the news about their rotation, he didn't want to get his hopes up.

Karissa's travel plans were all set. She was flying out to visit her parents the week before Christmas. She had enough vacation time available and the office was deserted between Christmas and New Year's anyway so the employees could be with their families.

She was excited to see her parents, but was more than a little sad since she still didn't know what timeframe Lane was coming back for. He didn't mention anything about rotating out yet, so she assumed there was nothing to tell.

The city was all decorated for Christmas and Karissa really tried to embrace the spirit of the holidays. It was tough because she really wanted to experience it all with Lane.

Terri had to wait until the school break to fly to Virginia to see her parents. From what she said, her parents were excited to meet Karissa but knew she and Lane had

some things to work out before that
happened.

Her letters to Lane were filled
with how much she missed him. He
said the same and she smiled every
time she read the words. She was so
in love with him, and although it
was crazy to her mind, her heart
seemed to be very sure.

Karissa and Terri met up two
days before she left for California so
they could exchange their Christmas
gifts. This time they met at Terri's
place.

Terri showed her the Christmas
cards she got from her students and
they were the right mix of cute and
sweet. The kids really liked to draw
pictures of themselves as Santa.

As soon as they sat down on
the sofa, Karissa gave Terri a look,
and asked, "Are you going to tell me

who has you looking so dreamy-eyed?"

To her credit, Terri blushed. "Well, I guess in an attempt to get back at me for setting him up with you, Lane decided to give my email address to his friend Kenston."

Surprised, Karissa raised her eyebrows but remained silent.

Nodding in agreement, Terri replied, "I know." She smiled, and continued, "Well, we hit it off. Honestly, I always thought he was kind of a chauvinistic, from what Lane said, but he is sweet and sensitive."

Happy for her friend, Karissa gave her a hug. "I guess we're both in the same boat then."

With a sigh, Terri nodded. "I know you don't have reliable internet at your parents' place all the time but I've got your cell number and their phone number so I'll call you if I hear anything."

Her friend's reassurance made Karissa feel better. "Please do," She said, then asked, "when you we eat?"

Lane was packing his bag when Kenston came into his room. The door was open so his friend didn't bother to knock. "Hey," Lane said to him. When Kenston didn't reply, Lane turned around to see his friend looking worried. "What's up?" Lane asked.

"I, uh," Kenston began. "I uh

sort of started writing to your sister and she invited me to come to Virginia to meet your parents over the holidays."

Surprised, Lane sat down at his desk. He had to think about this for a minute. "Wow," he said.

Kenston walked over and sat down on the cot so he was facing Lane. "I promise, Huff, I'll never hurt her intentionally. I feel different when I read her words," he paused, trying to find the words, "grounded, I guess."

Smiling, Lane clapped his friend on the shoulder and said, "Well, maybe I'll have a valid reason to call you brother from now on." He was glad if his sister and his friend found happiness.

"Were you able to get everything set?" Kenston asked as he stood up.

Nodding, Lane stood and zipped up his bag. "Yep, all set."

His eyebrows raised, Kenston mumbled, "Never thought I'd see you as a recruiter."

Karissa arrived at the Reno Airport. The place was packed with skiers and holiday travelers all trying to get to their destinations.

Her parents were picking her up so she didn't have to rent a car and make the six-hour drive to Bishop, her home town, by herself.

She was going down to the baggage claim area when she saw her parents. They were waving and smiling at her.

Her mother reached her first, giving her a hug, and saying, "You are too pale to be living in a southern state."

Karissa laughed because her mom always said that to her. "Hi mom," she returned. Stepping over to her dad, she gave him a big hug too.

"Hello, munchie," Her dad said, using her childhood nickname he'd given her as a little girl.

They got Karissa's bags, her father making the obligatory grumbling that women packed too much in their suitcases.

The drive to Bishop was filled

with catching up on the lives of old friends and family members.

A little bummed that her brother, Mark, and sister, Katie, weren't going to make it this year, Karissa just smiled. They were going to their respective in-laws' houses.

Karissa's mom was an expert at keeping tabs on everyone. She was never without friends and always enjoyed her life. Listening to her mother talk about her latest volunteer endeavors, Karissa wondered if she would ever be that open.

Not surprisingly, her mind drifted to Lane. She prayed he was alright. Since she was traveling, she sent hm an email just before she left for the airport, explaining that she wouldn't be able to email him until this evening.

With the change in hours, they arrived back at the house in the early evening. Karissa sighed as she got out of the vehicle. Lord, her parents went all out with the holiday decorating and it was purely blissful to see their house.

Her father was a master with woodworking so he made these huge figures for the yard. They were always trimmed with little, colorful Christmas lights and glowed in the waning daylight.

"Wow, Dad," Karissa said as she stood just outside the SUV and stared at the expansive yard decorations.

Clint Godfried smiled, and told his daughter, "Don't look at me, I just do the heavy lifting. Your mother is the mastermind."

Smiling at her husband, Blaire Godfried walked around the vehicle and gave her husband a hug, saying, "And I appreciate all the heavy lifting you do."

Watching her parents, as they hugged, the glow of the Christmas lights backlighting their shape, Karissa prayed that she and Lane would have the kind of love her parents had.

The three of them walked inside and Karissa could smell her mother's cookies. She was transported to wonderful memories of her childhood, baking with her mom for the holidays.

Blaire was very insistent on making sure all of her neighbors received cookie platters and told Karissa, and her siblings, "The best gifts are the ones that come from the heart." It was an awesome memory and had her thinking of Lane.

"Sweetheart," Blair frowned at her daughter, "what are you thinking so hard about?"

Deciding now was as good time as any, Karissa answered, "Can we sit down, I have a story to tell the two of you." Once they sat down, she proceeded to tell them about Lane. She told them everything she could think of and everything she felt.

Chapter 15

Lane was on the plane, sitting next to Kenston, and getting more agitated by the second. He'd been an idiot again and didn't tell Karissa that they were on their way back to the states.

She was on her way to her parents' house for the holidays and he didn't know where they lived. Not to mention, he had no way of knowing if they knew about him, so he didn't feel comfortable just showing up. But, with all of that, he wasn't sure how he'd managed to wait until she got back to Houston to see her.

"Will you stop," Kenston nudged Lane out of his thoughts. "You're thinking so hard that I can hear the gears in your head turning. Geez, we got this."

Shooting his friend a nasty look, Lane wasn't sure who had what but he didn't feel like he had anything at the moment.

The next day, their plane finally landed in Virginia.

Everyone was given two weeks' leave and told when to report back to the base.

Since Lane already put in for his orders to do recruiting, he didn't even listen to half of what was being said.

As he and Kenston walked out of the Admin building on the base, they saw Terri standing by her car, waving excitedly.

It only took a few seconds for Lane to figure out that the sparkle in his sister's eyes wasn't reserved for him. He looked at Kenston, smiled, and said, "Go ahead." He stayed where he was to let Kenston run over and hug Terri while he spun her around.

The joy on Terri's face was priceless and Lane prayed Karissa would have the same look when they finally met in person.

Stepping back from Kenston, Terri opened her arms to give her brother a hug, and whispered, "Welcome home," in his ear.

Lane squeezed his sister tightly, then leaned back so he could see her face. He smiled while he looked over at Kenston, then to his sister. "So, this is what you meant by 'we'."

Nodding, Kenston clapped Lane on the back, and told him, "A

plan is in motion, no worries."

They got into the car, with Terri driving, Kenston in the passenger seat, and Lane in the backseat. Not sure how he felt about not being the focus of his sister's attention, Lane tried not to sulk.

"Okay," Terri started to explain as soon as they went through the exit gate on the base, "We're going to drive to Mom and Dad's house now." She looked into the rearview mirror to make eye contact with her brother, and added, "They want to make sure you're really alright." She smiled, "Plus, I want them to meet Aaron." She reached across the counsel and took Kenston's hand into hers. "Then, on the 23rd, we're flying to Reno, Nevada since that's the closest airport to where Karissa's parents live. She saw the look of surprise on her brother's face, and continued, "Then, on Christmas Eve you're going to find her and make you both very happy."

Lane wanted to cry, he was so grateful to Terri and Kenston for making the arrangements. "Thank you," He mouthed to his sister.

Karissa was enjoying the brisk morning air, sitting on the front porch of her parents' house with a mug of hot cocoa and watching the deer in the distance. They got food from feeders her dad put out for them.

Her mother joined her and sat

down, before asking, "How did you sleep?"

Even after being here for almost a week, Karissa couldn't seem to settle herself down. She was relieved when her parents took the story of how she and Lane got together in a good way. They actually told her they thought it was romantic and told Karissa to follow her heart.

"I'm okay, I guess," She came out of her thoughts and answered her mom's question.

Blaire winked at her daughter, and asked, "Is it because you're excited that Santa is coming?"

It was difficult not to feel the excitement of the holiday season when she was around her mother.

"Maybe," Karissa answered, but she suspected they both knew it wasn't true.

Blaire took a sip of her coffee, and asked, "Did you get an email this morning?"

Karissa nodded, yes, and said, "Yes, but it was short." She sighed and took a sip of the hot cocoa before adding, "I'm grateful to hear from him so I don't know why I'm being so sullen."

Reaching over, and grasping her daughter's hand, Blaire told her, "You're not being sullen, you're being in love. There is a difference." She gave Karissa's hand a quick squeeze, and then suggested, "Why don't you pray about it and see what happens."

Watching her mom get up and go into the house to start making breakfast, Karissa thought about how she really hadn't prayed about her and Lane. Maybe it was time to place it in someone else's hands for a change.

Lane hugged his parents, thanked them for understanding that he and Terri wouldn't be staying for Christmas.

His mother said it was fine but she expected everyone to come to Virginia next year. She also handed Lane a small box and explained it was her grandmother's wedding rings. When Lane opened it, the thought it was perfect and hugged his mom again for being so generous and awesome.

Lane, Kenston, and Terri

boarded the plane a couple of hours later. He spent the flight rolling his eyes a million times while watching Terri and "Aaron" as they made goo goo eyes at one another. He was jealous, and he'd be the first one to admit it.

Their plane got in a little late and it took a fair amount of time for their bags to get offloaded at baggage claim. Since it was so late, they were relieved that they'd already made plans to stay over night in Reno. They would head down to Bishop first thing the next morning.

As Kenston drove the rental car to the hotel, Terri called Karissa's mother. She wanted to confirm that they were okay with people just showing up. Terri had never met them in person before but assured Lane they would be up for it.

A half hour later, she hung up the phone, gave the guys a thumbs up, and said, "We are a go."

The nerves started running through Lanes veins now. It was one thing to think all of this in his head, but quite another to actually put the plan into action and surprise Karissa on Christmas Eve.

According to Terri's intel, Karissa did tell her parents about their relationship so at least they weren't blindsided. From what Terri said, Karissa's parents were very happy for them and were excited to be in on the surprise.

Christmas Eve morning, Karissa woke up early. She didn't

know why, but she found herself wide awake. The sun was barely up over the horizon. She stretched out, put on her favorite fuzzy socks, and quietly walked out to the kitchen.

She started getting out the ingredients and bowls. She was lost in her task so she didn't hear her mom walk to the doorway of the kitchen. When she did notice her mom, she said, "Morning, Mom."

Smiling, Blaire asked, "I was wondering if you'd remember to do that?" They had a tradition of making chocolate chip coffee cakes on Christmas Eve so everyone had something to eat on Christmas morning. "Uh," Her mom said, "we need to make an extra one this year."

Surprised, Karissa nodded out

and got out another pan. Apparently, they were delivering the coffee cakes to someone at church or a neighbor.

Karissa and her mom worked quietly until the coffee cakes were in the oven. Then, they decided to make breakfast for today.

When her dad joined them, her mother turned on the Christmas music and asked him to go out to the shed for more firewood.

Clint nodded, but motioned for Karissa to come with him.

As they walked out to get wood from the pile, Clint asked his daughter, "So you really love this Lane guy."

Lost in the sounds of their boots crunching in the snow, it took a few moments for Karissa to process the question. She smiled, and answered, "Yes dad, he makes me feel like I imagine you make mom feel."

"We just want you to be happy," Clint told her, and wrapped his arms around her for a hug. He knew that later today, he was going to lose her a little bit to someone else, and it made him sad and happy at the same time.

After breakfast, Karissa and her parents went around the area delivering baked good to the neighbors, wishing everyone a Merry Christmas.

Every house they went to was friendly and open, and Karissa felt like she was around extended family.

Her mother insisted they go to the earlier Christmas Eve service this year, saying that she needed to wrap some last-minute gifts she'd forgotten about. Looking over at her dad, who just shrugged, Karissa agreed. Usually, they went to the midnight service but this year was a little different.

The church service was lovely. Karissa loved lighting the candles and singing the carols. She said a special prayer for Lane and his friends.

When her father pulled into the driveway at their house, Karissa noticed a car parked there. She asked her mother, "Were you expecting anyone?"

Blaire nodded, "Yes, my cousins decided to come over, that's why I had to get the last-minute gifts."

Nodding, Karissa sat back and waited for her dad to park their Jeep before getting out. Her mother had a very big extended family so having more people here would be fun. Maybe it would help her not think about Lane so much.

Going into the house first, Karissa called out, "Hello."

Expecting family, Karissa almost fainted when Terri came out of the dining room doorway and yelled, "Merry Christmas!"

The two of them hugged

tightly, trying to hold back the tears.

"What are you doing here?" She asked Terri, confused.

Terri acted like she was thinking hard about the answer, then said, "Santa asked me to help him out this year," she smiled at Karissa, "you've been a really good girl and he wanted you to have a special gift."

Karissa's smile faded; excitement bubbled up in her chest. "Is he here?" she asked Terri.

As soon as Terri nodded, Karissa's head felt like it might explode. "Oh my Lord," She said and leaned against her dad as he came up beside her.

Looking over at her mom, Karissa felt he tears well in her eyes.

Blaire said, "It's okay, go say hello."

Lane and Aaron were joking about a snowball fight when they noticed a woman standing in the doorway of the house.

Aaron spoke first, saying, "I guess that's my cue to go inside and meet Karissa's parents." He patted Lane's shoulders, and told him, "Good luck."

Lane couldn't speak so he only nodded.

One of the two men standing outside walked toward the house and Karissa saw it was Kenston. She smiled and nodded toward him.

Kenston said, "We'll do the

formal stuff later, you've got better things to do," before passing her to go inside the house.

Karissa stayed where she was and stared at Lane, who started moving toward the house, but stopped. She figured it would be up to her to move first. She walked down the steps and toward him.

When she was about two feet away from him, Karissa started crying, and whispered, "Lane."

Lane's eyes couldn't get enough of her. She was the most beautiful woman in the world. "Karissa," he whispered back and stepped forward to take her into his arms.

"Oh my gosh," She cried into his coat and held onto him tightly.

They stood where they were, just holding one another. Neither one knew, nor cared, how long.

Karissa reluctantly pulled away first. She wanted to look into his eyes. She'd memorized them from his pictures but they were more beautiful in person. "How?" She asked him.

Lane pointed back toward the house, "With a lot of help from our elves."

Not bothering to turn around, Karissa knew her parents, Terri, and Kenston were at the window, watching them.

"You're here," Karissa whispered, not sure when the reality would sink in.

Looking at her beautiful eyes, Lane answered, "I'm here." He leaned forward to kiss her.

The kiss held all the tenderness and love both of them were building for the last seven months.

Karissa knew it was going to be her last "first kiss" and was happier than she could ever be.

When Lane ended the kiss, he said, "Before we go inside, and have to deal with the rest of them, I wanted you to know that I'm in love with you, Karissa Godfried. You've gotten me thought everything this year."

Smiling through her tears, Karissa responded, "Back at you, sweet man."

Lane pulled the box from his mother out of his pocket and knelt down in the snow. "And I don't want to be without you again, so I'm asking you under the stars, on Christmas Eve, to give me your heart and love for the rest of our lives together."

Karissa nodded, and replied, "My mom always said the best gifts were from the heart, and you've got my heart, for now and always, Staff Sergeant Huff."

Sliding the ring on her finger, Lane sent up a silent prayer that they would always be as happy as they were right then. He stood up and walked with his fiancé into the house.

The party was already starting.

And if anyone were to look inside that house, they would see love and laughter, and a Merry Christmas was had by all.